Buried HEARTS

C.E. JOHNSON

Cover design: Sarah Hansen, Okay Creations
www.okaycreations.com
Interior Design: Jill Sava, Love Affair With Fiction
www.loveaffairwithfiction.com
Editor: Shannon A. Thompson
www.shannonathompson.com

Want to know what's coming up next?
To stay up to date on all new release information:
http://bit.ly/CEJohnsonNewsletter

BURIED HEARTS

In the Dark Series #3

—

C.E. JOHNSON
-2019-

Dedication

—

To my sweet Sophie girl
who was attached to my right side for thirteen years.

May you rest over the Rainbow Bridge,
taking deep breaths and sleeping under all the blankets.
I miss you fiercely.

Chapter
One

—

Paul

The scent that drifts within the atmosphere on Wednesday nights is different than any other night in O'Reilly's pub. It's only nights like tonight, when the traditional smell of wood and hops transforms to stagnant, suffocating air. Death. It smells like death.

Every other day of the week, I manage to save face. My short brown hair gets tamed with gel. My suits are crisply pressed and shoes are free from scuffs. And my mind is strictly devoted to Knoxx Developments. But Wednesdays after five in the evening, none of that matters. It's like an internal alarm sounds and I lose the ability to care about any of it. All I want to do is sit on a stool and forget.

My usual spot at the far end of the L-shaped bar is as empty as the crater in the center of my chest. "Paul." Kael nods in my direction as he passes by with his hands full of beer. As one of the owners of this pub and the brother of one of my best friends, Kael has seen me on many Wednesday nights. He knows better than to pick up a conversation, so he says hello and continues on his business. The click of my dress shoes on the old wood floors echo in my ears as I walk to my seat.

I don't see Tasha or Daphne behind the bar like I usually do. In fact, there's no one behind the bar. Pressing back with my feet against the dark metal foot rails, the stool tilts back, giving me a view straight down the hallway toward the kitchen and offices. Her brown hair swings out of the door before she does and, internally, I scream a little. The front two feet of the bar stool slam down onto the wood floor as my hand slowly rubs down my face in defeat before she ever opens her mouth.

"Hopefully someday soon, you find better use of your Wednesday nights," Sophie snips as she swings her body around the bar.

"I really need to find a new pub."

I'm one of the luckiest assholes there is. I have a group of people who care so much for me. Benson and I have been friends since we were kids. When he and Sophie got married, Sophie became like a sister to me. If it wasn't for Sophie, I would have never met Finn or Kael O'Reilly, who own this pub. Daphne worked at O'Reilly's for a long time before marrying Finn and becoming part owner as well. She still works behind the bar regularly and, since I come in here regularly, we've spent a lot of time together. Daphne doesn't usually bust my balls for being in here. Sophie, on the other hand, has no problems telling me exactly what she thinks. Even though they all can get on my last nerve, I'm thankful for each one of them. They're the only reason I haven't ended up in jail. Again.

"Go ahead. But I promise you, no one will bail your ass out when you cause a ruckus in someone else's bar."

"What are you doing here?" It was an accident that those words came out of my mouth a bit harsh.

She spins around from the computer screen and looks at me like she wants to knock my ass right off this stool. "It's nice to see you too."

"I didn't mean it like that, Soph." Her stern face turns soft as she huffs and even manages to flash me a quick smile. "Benson didn't tell me you two were coming into town. I wasn't expecting to see you. Where's Daphne?"

"She went to visit her parents for a few days. You want a water? How about a soda?"

"Nice try. Whiskey. Reach high."

Sophie rolls her eyes and reaches for the Paddy Irish Whiskey. After pouring a shit amount into a square glass and placing it in front of me, she leans onto the bar. "I think you should talk to someone, Paul. Maybe they can help you sort your—"

The glass slams onto the bar with force after I poured its smoky sweet contents down my throat. "I know you think you're helping me right now. I don't need it. I'm fine."

"If you would just talk about it…"

A sharp breath exits my mouth as I hop backward off the stool. I just got here, and if this is how the night is going to go, there are plenty of places that sell whiskey in this city.

"Don't go," she says. After she watches me sit back down, she rolls her eyes, pours a little more into the glass, then begins to walk away. "You are just as stubborn as Benson. The two of you are one of a kind."

"Hey," I shout to her as I straddle back onto the stool. "Leave the bottle."

Because Sophie is here and I don't want the extra headache of her preaching to me about getting completely hammered, I don't engulf my drinks like I usually do. After having a few, I tap on the bar to get Sophie's attention.

"Don't take my glass. I'll be right back."

She nods while tending to the other customers who are belly up to the best Irish Pub in Boston. With the college not far, on Friday and Saturday nights this place is hopping with young college kids. Thankfully, O'Reilly's has been getting popular with an older crowd during the week. Halfway to the bathroom, I run into Finn coming out of the office.

"Hey, you look exceptionally sober this evening." Finn grins.

"I almost forgot how funny you are. Sophie's been up there busting my balls."

"And look at the good it's done you. How refreshing not to have to restrain you on a Wednesday." Finn pats me on the shoulder as he snickers past me.

"I need to find a new bar."

"I heard that, asshole," Finn shouts from behind me. Then I hear, "Firecracker! Be nice."

I can't help but laugh. He knows just as well as I do that no one on this earth could tell that woman what to do unless she wants them to.

As I come around the corner, returning from my bathroom trip, a bright purple shirt catches my eye from the bar stool closest to the front door. It's been a long time since we were in high school together. But I would recognize those eyes anywhere. The color so light brown they almost look gold. My stomach falls as I look at her. She was my first love. My first heartache. My first everything, and I was hers. But we were just young and dumb. We never had a chance. She's just as gorgeous as the first time I laid eyes on her walking down the school hallway. I'm shook as a man passes by me to the bathroom, and I realize that with one small movement she could be looking right at me. I quickly dodge into the booth closest to me to avoid being seen.

"Paul, what the hell are you doin' hiding in the booth?" Finn's devious grin only irritates me further. I do not need this shit tonight. One night a week. That's all I ask for. I work from sun up until long past the sun sets every other day. Work. Eat. Sleep. Repeat. Every day except for the day created by the devil himself that starts with a W. One night is all I want to drown my pain in the bottom of a bottle in a place that I feel safe. Knowing that Finn isn't going to let this go, I let out a heavy sigh.

"See that chick over there?"

Finn follows the direction of my finger to the curvy brunette at the far side of the bar. "Yeah, I see her."

"Let's just say she's not my biggest fan."

Finn's evil grin widens. I instantly regret telling him anything. Finn has become one of my best friends and one of the very few people I trust with my life. But that doesn't mean that he also isn't one of the biggest assholes I know. I flop my head onto my hand and wait for whatever smart ass comment that no doubt is coming my way.

"Smart girl," he quips.

"Will you grab my glass from the bar?" I point to where I was sitting before.

"Fill it up, I assume?" Finn asks.

"Just bring me the damn bottle."

I've been nursing the liquid in my glass for quite some time now. The sight of her is so distracting that I've barely been able to move my eyes around this bar. As the time passed, Jolene went from bright eyed, to worried, to not giving a fuck. When I first saw her, she was checking her watch repeatedly. Every time the front door would squeak open, she would spin around to see who was walking in the pub. After a while, she stopped doing all of those things, and now the shots are disappearing from her glass quicker than Sophie can put them in front of her. A small part of me is curious and wants to go to her. The feeling only lasts for a few seconds before I remember how much of a bad idea that would be. A vision of the past fills my head. My eyes close from the pain I can still see in those gorgeous eyes of hers. The pain that I put there.

"Paul? Are you okay?"

Sophie's voice catches my attention and my eyes shoot open. I didn't hear her approach the booth I seem to be cowering in like a little bitch.

"Of course I am. Why?"

"You never sip your drinks like that. I mean it's a good thing. But what's the deal?"

"That girl over there downing the shots?" Sophie looks in the direction of my finger, then nods, looking puzzled. "I know her." I take what's left of the amber liquid in my glass and down it.

"So why don't you go talk to her? She got stood up by some asshole tonight."

"Nope. No fucking way. I'm not in the mood for that thrashing tonight."

Sophie slides into the booth across from me and throws her bar towel on the table. She leans back and crosses her arms. I know what that means. She's going to hound me for details. By now, you would think the questions would end. I never give details.

"What did you—?"

"I'm not talking about this. I don't beg, but I will ask you nicely not to inform her that I'm sitting over here. When she leaves, I'll go home."

Sophie huffs as she gets out of the booth, trying to act annoyed. The kind smile she flashes me before she heads back up to the bar confirms that she won't say anything. At least not to Jolene. I would bet money that Benson will hear all about this before I even make it home tonight.

The later it gets in the evening, the more unstable Jolene becomes on the barstool. I haven't touched the bottle in front of me since Finn placed it there two hours ago other than the first fill up. Sophie stopped serving her liquor and instead placed a cup of coffee in front of her. I try to stay occupied on my phone, but my senses are heightened when a man comes precariously close to her. I slide closer to the edge of the booth to get a better visual of him. My eyes flick to Sophie, who has also become hyper aware of the man. Sophie has been working this bar for a long time. Her instincts are almost as sharp as mine. Almost. When the man leans further into Jolene, she leans in the other direction. That hesitation was the only thing Sophie needed to move into action. Finn has a rule in his pub that you only intervene if it's absolutely necessary. There are a lot of dirt bags in this world and, as much as we would like to make every one of them our business, we just can't. All we can do is our best and protect those who want to be protected. However, once Sophie found out that I know Jolene, she was being looked out for whether she wanted it or not. Sophie moves closer to Jolene and begins talking to the man, who has also had quite enough alcohol for the evening. My line of vision is briefly blocked by two women heading to the bathroom, but the second I get a clear shot, I read his lips say, "Fuck you" to Sophie. She spins and shoots me a murderous expression as the man wraps one of his arms around Jolene's waist.

I lock my eyes on Jolene's reluctant expression as my rigid body rises from the booth and marches straight for him.

"Easy, Paul." I hear Sophie shout as I come toe to toe with a man who can't be over twenty-five.

"You know her?" I ask him.

"What business is it of yours?"

Ah, to be young and stupid again. This guy has no idea who he's dealing with. I guess I probably don't look like much to some people. My casual business suit doesn't really scream *I can kill you with one hand.*

"It isn't. She's hot though, huh?"

His only response to my bait is raising his eyebrows and licking his lip in her direction. She drunkenly giggles, but tries to back away from him.

"What's her name?" I ask. The smirk on my face isn't there because I think he's brilliant. It's there because my fingernails are digging into the palm of my hand and the release is going to feel so fucking good.

"Who cares? Am I right?" His laughter only lasts a half a breath before my hand connects with his face. It was a reaction that even I wasn't fully ready for. Jolene takes a small stumble to the side and I reach out, grabbing her elbow to steady her. Seeing how drunk she is makes me want to punch the kid again.

"Goddamnit, Paul. There's blood all over my floor," Finn says, sounding bored as he jogs up to me. "You could have at least brought him out front. Who's going to clean this shit up?"

One of the man's buddies helps him get off the floor as he continues to hold his hand to his busted lip. Finn pulls him in close and speaks quietly into his ear. The kid's eyes get wide as he shakes his head. Finn pats him on the back, hands him a wad of paper towels for his face, then shows him the door. Finn's threats are never to be taken lightly. I haven't a clue about what he said and truly it's none of my business. Luckily, he didn't argue. Finn is much nicer than I am, and that's saying something, because Finn's "nice" isn't really nice at all.

"Sorry for the mess, man. Give me something to clean it up."

"I'll get it. You get her home."

The sudden shock of what I'm about to have to do sets in. Not only did I not want Jolene to notice that I was in this bar with her, now I have to take her home too. I turn to Jolene to see her beautiful golden eyes staring at me. Her tanned olive skin is glistening from the spilled beer that she was sprayed with when I knocked it out of the asshole's hand. She's absolutely mesmerizing. Just like she always was. And that's what I'm afraid of.

"Paul? Whtr ya doin' her?" Her slurred speech is a hopeful indication that by morning, she won't remember seeing me at all.

"Just taking you home."

"Nah, I'm gon drive mysef."

"The fuck you are."

Her delayed reaction from the liquor gives me ample time to grab the car keys out of her purse and stick them in my pocket. Sophie hands her the cellphone she had laying on the bar and she shoves it into her handbag just before she teeters back into me. Never did I think that my arms would be holding onto Jolene Barrington again. If she were in her right mind, I would probably be icing my balls. And I wouldn't blame her one bit.

"C'mon, shot queen," I tease.

She gives me a scrunched up mocking face before stumbling toward the front door. This wasn't supposed to happen tonight. It's Wednesday for fuck sakes. I get one night that I can sulk in a bottle of Irish whiskey and get so drunk that I forget my own name. Now, not only does my chest still feel like the empty cavity it does on every other day of the week, I've got a new pain. This one is in my ass and its name is Jolene.

A hand on my shoulder squeezes as Finn stops me just before I clear the door.

"What's up with you two?" He nods in the direction of Jolene swaying on the sidewalk.

"We dated a long time ago. Other than that, nothing." I smack Finn on his bicep and turn around to see Jolene hunched over a trash can. Finn's laugh disappears as the door shuts.

My body leans against the light pole next to her as I wait for her to finish emptying her stomach. The temperature outside is still chilly for late spring. The breeze flows through the buttons of my shirt and gives me the cool down I need.

"Feel better?" Her head barely shakes to the side as she wipes her mouth. "C'mon."

I forgot how small Jolene's hand felt when it was in mine. It's hard not to think of the last time I held her as we walk to my car. Some people rarely remember their high school years. I remember them well. Especially the one that Jolene was in. She practically falls into the passenger seat. That was much easier than I thought it would be. As I round the front of the car, I see her wipe under both of her eyes. Part of me wants to know everything. Why was she in O'Reilly's? Who was she meeting and why are they worth the tears about to fall? There's so many questions running through my mind. But as I get in the driver's side and look to her mascara-streaked teary eyes, I remember that it's none of my fucking business.

"Where do you live?"

"You 'member my parents' house?"

"Yes."

"There."

"When did you—"

"After my ex-husband ffffuckin' left me."

I'll remember not to bring that up again. If fire could have shot out of her mouth and burned down the entire city, we would all be ash laying in the streets.

I had heard through mutual acquaintances that Jolene had gotten married. The same ones informed me about her divorce a few years later. I began to avoid them so I would stop hearing more about Jolene's life. After what I did to her, it was far from my business to know any of it.

The streetlights cast shadows through the window as we pass them on the way to her parents' house. I get a glimpse of her left hand sitting on her thigh and notice the tan line still remains where her wedding ring sat on her finger.

"Sorry. I heard about—"

Snoring interrupts my attempt at sensitivity. The fact that Jolene just passed out isn't what bothers me, but knowing that I might not be able to wake her ass back up does. I do not want to step foot in that house. How in the hell did I get myself into this shit?

The familiar brownstone in Beacon Hill sits right outside the passenger window.

"Jo." I shake her gently, trying to wake her. "Jolene," I yell. Nothing. Even with the slam of my car door, not even a twitch of an eyelid. Coming to the conclusion that I'm going to have to carry her into the house, I pull her keys out of my pocket and go up to the front door. Pressing my ear to the cool steel, there is silence from the inside. I lean far over the iron rail and look into the living room window for any lights on, but everything is dark. Like a toddler, I throw a mini tantrum in my head for having to go inside. Under the light from the porch, I find the only key on the ring that doesn't belong to a car and open the front door a crack. Then I stomp back to the car and open the passenger side. Jolene's body slumps out of the car and into my arms. Other than a tiny moan, she situates her head onto my shoulder, and I kick the car door shut. Damn her for smelling like sugar. Whatever perfume she has on smells like a fucking cupcake. My mouth begins salivating thinking about it. This night is getting worse as it goes on.

As quietly as I can, I push open the front door and head straight for the living room couch. There's no way I want to get caught in here by her parents. They despised me then. I know that hasn't changed. Just as I place Jolene on the couch, she starts coughing loudly. Sure. After everything I did to wake her, she wakes up now.

"Shhhh. Don't wake up your parents. You're at home. Sleep it off," I whisper.

I'm halfway out of the house before I turn back to see Jolene sitting up on one arm, hair wild and half in her face.

"You're shhhhtill and azzhole," she mumbles before lying back down on the couch.

I step lightly on my way out and silently shut the front door. Once on the stoop, memories of being a kid from the wrong side of town standing in this spot hit me. Back then, the tree-lined streets and iconic brownstones were vastly different than the home I would go back to. It was no surprise that Jolene's father didn't want us together. She was the only daughter of a wealthy doctor and I was the poor kid with a rap sheet. I never would have imagined that things would turn out the way they did.

—

I fling my car keys onto the island in my obnoxious condo that Benson made me get. He said I should embrace the life that I've made for myself. Whatever that means. I open the fridge, grab a cold beer and sit in my lonely cold space. I have the basics. A table to eat at, a bed to sleep in, a couch and TV to unwind. That's about it. Some could say I live a minimalist lifestyle. It's easier to let them think that I'm really into the modern way of living than to tell them the truth. I spend my days creating beautiful homes for people. People who are going to share them with others they love. I have found my calling in designing spaces in great detail for those who want to live out their family dreams in the heart of this city. But I'm a realist, and that dream isn't going to come true for me.

Each shoe falls to the floor as I kick them off and take a long swig from my beer. Looking around my empty, dark apartment some days is suffocating. The nothingness feeds the hungry demon in my soul. After everything I've done and the love I've lost, nothing is exactly what I deserve. My phone chimes just like it does every Thursday at midnight. Finally, it's not Wednesday anymore. I lean further into the couch when a sharp pinch in my leg through my pants takes me by surprise. My muscles go limp as my fingers wrap around the keys in my pocket. Jolene's keys. I had put them back in my pocket after I unlocked her front door. I guess this means that it doesn't matter if she completely forgets seeing me tonight. She's about to see me again tomorrow. And she'll be sober. Fuck my life.

Chapter
Two

—

Jolene

Regardless of the massive headache that is radiating through my skull at the moment, all I can think about is getting a big greasy cheeseburger. What is it about hangovers and fast food that just seems to go hand in hand? Years ago I could tip back drink after drink and it would hardly affect me. Obviously, times have changed and I can't handle my liquor like I used to. I pop two aspirin and down a cup of water. From the kitchen, I can see the disheveled blanket on the couch. I have no idea how I got there last night. I toss the now empty water bottle into the trash and lean against the counter to wait for the coffee to finish brewing. It's quiet. So quiet that I can hear my own ears ringing. They say that when your ears ring, someone is talking about you. It wouldn't surprise me. I'm a fucking mess. Hell, I'm still in the same goddamned clothes I went out in last night.

A knock at my front door startles me, causing me to pour way too much sugar into my coffee. I hate overly sweet coffee, and now I'll have to wait for more to brew. This day is already not off to a great start. If I knew what's good for me, I would ignore the door and go up to bed. Being that I have never been very good at listening to reason, the curiosity wins, and I head to the front of the house.

Through the small opening in the door I don't see anyone on the stoop. I pull it open further, peek my head out, and nearly choke on my spit. Seeing him leaning against the side rail of my stoop in his casual black suit isn't a sight I could have ever predicted. I'd say I was hallucinating if I didn't know better. Age has done Paul Kovette well. I've seen him once or twice around town, but I made sure to dodge out of his line of vision before he saw me. Now here he stands. On the very stoop that my world crashed down on. Or at least that's how it felt back then. The first thing I notice is his stylish appearance. His brown hair is short on the sides, and the longer hair on the top is styled loosely back. His sharp jawline is covered in a manicured five o'clock shadow. My eyes travel down his long legs, which cross at the ankles as he leans against the iron railing. A hint of his bicep bulge shows through the sleeve of his suit jacket as he clutches onto something. I wish I could see his eyes, but the mirrored aviators are only showing my reflection. A flutter of nervousness mixes in with the nausea in my stomach. Those kinds of feelings have no place in my life right now. I clear my throat, stand tall, and prepare to get rid of him.

"What the hell do you want?"

Paul doesn't say anything, but lifts a fast-food bag in one hand and my car keys in his other hand. The events of last night slowly start coming back. I swallow hard and try to remember the words that came out of my mouth. I pray that I didn't tell him that I forgive him. Or that my heart missed a beat when I saw him outside of the city building a few months ago. Not after what he's done. Not after the way he left things.

"Forgot I had your keys in my pocket last night."

"Sure you did." My arms fold across my chest. "You took them on purpose, so I'd have to look at your arrogant face again today."

"Oh c'mon, Fancy."

"Don't you dare call me that."

I snatch my keys out of his hand and slam the door. He has some nerve coming around here. Of all the people in this city, how the hell did he stumble upon me last night? We haven't spoken in years, and now all of the sudden, there he is to swoop in and save the day? My brain begins turning rapidly. I remember how he used to keep an eye on me back when we were dating. *Is he having me watched?* Fire builds within me as the anger grows just thinking about it. I throw the door open to see the sack of food left on my stoop and the back of Paul's head walking down the sidewalk.

"Get back here," I yell.

Paul stops walking, but doesn't turn around right away. He stares straight ahead for a minute before he twists his head to look back. I'd be lying if his strong-angled jawline didn't remind me of how gorgeous he is. But I'm a little shocked to see a hint of pain in his face before he expertly wipes it clean again. That was always one of Paul's problems. It was impossible to get him to open up.

"Come here," I say.

Slowly, he turns his whole body around and looks to the ground as he makes his way back to me. Both hands are in his pants pockets, and his suit jacket is pulled away from his torso on each side, revealing the light blue button up under it. Watching his natural swagger as he walks toward me, I don't know how women aren't throwing themselves at him. He takes each step at a snail's pace until he is face to face with me. He glances up and his dark brown eyes come in contact with mine. For a moment, it's hard to remember what I want to say. Here we are, standing in front of each other after all this time and neither of us can speak. We just stare and it's like I'm looking into a time machine. My heart beats fast as I remember how much I once loved him. How much I once trusted him. How, at one time, I thought the two of us would disappear into the horizon of adventure. Paul breaks eye contact first and he turns to look down the street. It only takes that split second for me to gather my strength and the anger to rise again.

"Are you having me followed?"

"Are you still drunk?" he laughs.

"Not funny."

Paul always had a contagious laugh. My lips begin to tip up, but I clear my throat, straighten my face, and look to him for an answer.

"I don't know what the hell you're talking about." Even though Paul looked far from comfortable, his body was relaxed.

"How did you know I would be at O'Reilly's Pub last night? You show up out of nowhere, and suddenly you're bringing me hangover food?" I don't realize that I'm yelling until my neighbor rushes her little girl into the house while giving me a death stare. "Come inside. I want to talk to you."

"No fucking way. You should be thanking me for showing up and bringing your drunk ass home. I didn't even want to step foot in this house in fear of reliving the 'you're a piece of shit and not good enough for our daughter' speech from your old man."

"He's not here."

Paul's smug grin spreads across his face. I kick the door backward with my foot and gesture for him to come inside. Reluctantly, he nods and walks past me into the house. Damn my parents for raising me with manners. I roll my eyes knowing that I need to say it. "Thank you for bringing me home last night." My teeth clench together the entire time.

"And?" Paul asks while gesturing to continue talking. Internally I'm facing a battle between wanting to kick him right where it counts and wanting to laugh because he's so ridiculous.

"Thanks for the food."

"You're welcome." His voice is low as he turns his face away. This conversation is getting too nonchalant. I need to bring it back to why the hell he's here, standing in my house. "Why did you get me food anyway, and how did you know I wanted greasy cheeseburgers?"

"Isn't that what you always eat the day after drinking? At least you used to. I just assumed that you still did and that maybe if I brought it, you wouldn't kick me in the balls when I dropped off your keys."

It's irritating how he could know the tiniest detail about me, and yet didn't know me enough to trust my heart. Paul removes his hands from his pockets and unbuttons his suit jacket. He sits in the armchair across the room from me. He's smart not to get too close. I set the bag of food down in the kitchen, then walk back into the living room to get some real answers out of him.

"Are you having your heathens watch me?" I blurt the question out.

"I swear, I'm not. I have no reason to." I saw his eyebrows dip into the center of his face. If I wouldn't know any better, it looked like it hurt him a little to say that.

"Then how, after all this time, did you just happen upon me and save the day? I think you forget how familiar I am with your tricks. I don't fall for your bullshit anymore. And I won't stand for being followed by thugs."

Paul pulls both sides of his suit jacket together as he rises from the chair. He buttons it again, then walks to the front door.

"Before you go accusing people of things, you may want to do a little digging first." He turns around to face me and half of his mouth is tilted upright. "It wouldn't have taken but one phone call to find out that one of my best friends owns O'Reilly's Pub. I'm there every Wednesday, Fancy." He opens the door and his smirk turns into a full smile. "Perhaps you are the one keeping tabs on me."

Paul walks out and shuts the door behind him. I walk into the kitchen with my mouth fully ajar, stunned. I grab the bag of food and throw it across the room. He has some nerve. Then again, he always has. He was the bad boy my father warned me to stay away from. I didn't listen. I was aching for adventure and something different than the planned out daily life my parents had kept for me. I got in more trouble with Paul than I ever did in my entire life. He always lived life on the edge of a cliff. I'll never forget the first time Paul called me Fancy. He convinced me to sneak out of the opera my parents made me go to and he brought me to a party one of his friends was having. Everyone was casually dressed in jeans and t-shirts. I was in a fancy red dress and stuck out amongst the crowd. Paul couldn't take his eyes off of me all night. Just thinking about that night and the way he looked at me makes me smile. Wait. No. I'm mad at him. *I hate him.* I shake that memory and warm feeling off, then plop down in the kitchen chair.

That bastard is not getting the last word. Not this time.

Chapter
Three

—

Paul

"I should have just stayed out of it."

"Yeah right, you saw someone getting taken advantage of. There's no way you would have stood by and watched that happen. Why does all the good shit happen when I'm gone?" Daphne asks. I knew as soon as Finn and his big mouth told her about last night, my phone would be ringing. "She must be special for you to be so protective of her. How do you know her?"

"I'm not going there. When do you come back?"

"Tomorrow. Why?" she asks.

"Want to make sure you'll be there on Wednesday. I can't handle another one with Sophie. I love her, but some days, her mothering can be a bit much."

"I get it. I'll be there. If you feel like talking before then, you know where I live."

"I'll talk to you later."

"I mean it, Paul. When you're ready, just talk to one of us. Any of us. Bye."

Daphne knows I'm not the kind of guy to spill his guts. Not to anyone. I've spent a lifetime with Benson. He's the closest thing I have to a brother. When Sophie came along, she fit right in. I knew the second that Benson wanted to keep her safe that he was done for. I know if there ever came a time that I felt like talking, they would both be there. And so would Daphne and Finn. Truth be told, I'd be lost without any of them.

For most of my life, Benson was one of my only friends. He came from a hard-working family that didn't forbid their son from hanging out with a kid like me. Instead, his parents welcomed me with open arms and they became a safe haven for me. Even after I got into more trouble. Even after Benson and I got into a fist fight and stopped talking to each other. Even after Heather.

———

The constant beeps and ringing of contractors and clients last all day. It's not uncommon for me to get a call from a number that I don't know. But rarely do I get text messages from them. So it catches me off guard when one of the texts with only a number but no name pops up.

> **JOLENE:** *You're the last man I would track down.*
> **JOLENE:** *And don't call me Fancy ever again. Makes you a hypocrite when you say it while you're wearing a tailored suit, asshole.*

Taken aback, I stare at my phone for a minute before laughter takes over my empty office. She still has that spicy side to her. The side that she works so hard to hide from the world. I'm quickly distracted as Tina comes through my speaker to announce my client is here for our meeting.

The day is typical. For me anyway. I stay long after the last employee leaves the office completing paperwork or anything else I can keep myself busy with. Usually, I still have a hard time going home. If that's even what you want to call the place. My avoidance of spending too much time in that condo is one of the main reasons I've stayed in such great shape. Tonight was one of those nights where the thought of that empty useless condo weighed heavy on my mind. I hit the gym, then grab some food. The only thing I look forward to at the end of a long day is my bed. The cool, crisp bed sheets are very different from the scratchy hand-me-down couch that I slept on for most of my childhood. I climb in knowing that tomorrow will be much of the same. Wash. Rinse. Repeat. Monotony has never been so comfortable.

My phone lights up from the nightstand. I already know its Benson checking in for the day. It's the same text every night.

BENSON: *Any problems?*

He gets the same response from me every night.

PAUL: *Nope.*

I click out of our conversation, and Jolene's text from earlier catches my eye again. Something begins to bubble up inside of me. Shit, I feel bad. I growl loudly as I begin pushing different letters on my phone's keyboard.

PAUL: *You were drunk and I needed to make sure you got home safely. I didn't think you would even remember and the keys were a mistake. It wasn't my intention to bring any of this shit back up for either of us. I'm sorry.*

I power off my phone because if I don't, it would go off all night from all the other workaholics in this town who never sleep.

—

"Paul." Kael nods as I walk through O'Reilly's to my usual Wednesday night stool. It's been a week since I saw Jolene. This fucked up brain I have won't stop thinking about her, though. Even more reason to make up for last week. As I take a seat on the hard, wooden stool, I look behind the bar hoping to find Daphne. Her puffy blond hair is the first thing I see as she pops up from under the bar with a few rags in her hand.

"Ahhh, there's my favorite weekly customer," she says with a smile.

"Glad to see you're back. Where's Finn?" I ask.

"He's in the office. Usual?"

I roll my eyes at her ridiculous question, and she knowingly smiles, then I tap the bar before heading back to the office.

"Hey, buddy," Finn says as I walk in. His fingers click quickly on the keyboard and he never takes his eyes off of the monitor. "How the fuck are ya'?"

"Wanted to pay for making a mess of your bar again, man. I'll pay for whatever damage I caused."

The clicking immediately stops and he turns his attention to me. He tries to cross his arms against his chest, but they just look like two logs that barely bend. Finn is a man who doesn't have the ability to hide his power. He's built to show it off. One of the benefits of this is most would never attempt to cross a man like Finn. On the other hand, there are men like me. I get the element of surprise when they realize my power. The look on their face when they realize how easily I can crush them is my favorite part.

"You better get the fuck outta here with that talk. Your money isn't good here and you know it. You want your one night to drink and ignore whatever the hell is eating away at your insides? Fine. I can't control you. But I can keep an eye on you in this pub. I just hope one day you can let this shit go."

"You don't understand. I can't."

This isn't what I wanted to talk about when I came in here. For the longest time, no one brought it up. Now it seems like it enters almost all conversations.

"Then make me understand. It's obvious that daily life is tough, but every other day of the week, I can talk to you. You seem to at least pretend to be happy." Finn leans into his desk and places his arms on it. They're probably too heavy for him to hold up anymore. "Then Wednesday comes and you walk into my pub like half of a person. I can try to ward off Sophie and Daphne for now. But it's not somethin' we're gonna ignore forever."

"Appreciate that. I don't want to go to another bar on Wednesdays, but I can't take the constant questions anymore. Plus I don't know anyone who has better entertainment."

It's easy to get Finn to change the subject. He's got Irish blood running through his veins, and the best way to distract him is to talk about his pub. He used to target the college kids, but as he gets older, I think he's thinking more and more like his old man. He prides himself on running a no-bullshit authentic pub. Finn is the happiest schmuck in the world when a customer walks in and orders a pint.

Finn's face twists. "I don't have no fuckin' entertainment."

"Tasha is all the entertainment I'll ever need."

A loud smack echoes in the office from Finn's hand hitting his forehead. He knows just as well as everyone else who frequents O'Reilly's that Tasha should have been let go a long time ago. She can't carry a tray with a toothpick on it without dropping it much less a tray full of food or drinks. It hasn't gotten any better with time either. It's not uncommon to see the regulars shift from one side of the booth to the other as Tasha walks by with a tray. The poor thing is just as sweet as can be, but man, she's got zero balancing skills. We all know there has to be more to Finn and Kael keeping her around. We just haven't figured out what that reason is yet.

—

The first burn is always the best. Its pleasant torture flows from the top of my throat all the way down through my chest. From my usual seat, I can see the entire bar. You would think that I would have seen her walk in. I didn't. So when she plops down on the stool right next to me, it's not my fault that the amber liquid ends up in my lap instead of in my mouth.

"I forgive you."

Jolene's eyes roll as her words come out like they were painful. An uncontrollable snicker releases from deep within my chest with Jolene's proclamation.

"What are you forgiving me for?"

"I forgive you for being the asshole you were born to be."

"Ouch." I turn to her with a smirk. Her eyes sink directly into mine and it becomes obvious this banter between us hasn't eased that sadness in her eyes. It was there the day I left, and it was there last week when she laid eyes on me in this pub.

"Since when do you apologize, anyway?"

"Why are you here?"

She pulls a silver hook from her handbag, places it on the bar, and then hangs her handbag from it in between us.

"I want to know what happened to you."

Any warmth the whiskey gave me drains from my face. Like I've just stepped out of a sauna into the Alaskan wilderness in the dead of winter. Thankfully, Daphne had set the bottle on the small ledge on the inside of the bar. I lean over, grab it, and pour myself an extra dose. I take a slow sip before returning to the conversation with Jolene.

"I'm not sure what you're talking about."

"I've never seen you so…miserable."

"Well, I can say ditto to that." With a bad feeling in my gut and the whiskey running smooth, I can already tell this is not going to be a conversation I want to have. "I'm pretty damn shocked you're living back with dear old daddy."

"My parents don't live there anymore."

Movement from behind the bar grabs my attention. Daphne walks up with an obnoxious smile on her face and her eyes dart between the two of us. "What can I get you?" she asks Jolene.

"Vodka and cranberry juice."

"Comin' up." Daphne's smile didn't fade even slightly during their entire conversation. Nor did it when she came back and placed the drink in front of her than made lovey eyes between Jolene and me. She finally got the hint to leave when I coughed and gave her the look.

"So you live in mommy and daddy's big ass place all by yourself?"

She sighs loudly. "My parents bought a house in Arizona when they retired. They had it up for sale, but took it off the market when I needed somewhere to stay while I figured shit out."

All of this casual conversation is overloading my system. My natural introversion can barely stand my day-to-day social job. Not to mention that she's fucking up my road to ignorant bliss again tonight.

"Don't you have anything better to do?"

"Still the closed-off, cold-hearted jerk, I see."

Her words sting like a hundred bees piercing my skin. But it doesn't matter. She never needs to know the truth. The truth never set me free. The truth locked me in an eternal prison and buried the key under a gravestone in the mountains. Turning to face her, I realize that she saw my flinch. What the hell is wrong with me? She straightens her back and pushes her belly against the rim of the dark wood bar.

"I'll just sit here and have my drink. When I'm done, I'll leave. You won't even have to talk to me," she says.

What harm can a drink or two do? I grab my glass and clink it into hers. She's already here and the truth is, if she left, I would be worried about whether she got home okay. *Shit.* The night doesn't get any better as it goes on. The fact that every one of my friends has walked past us at one point with a shitty grin on their face tells me that when Jolene leaves, it won't be the end of her name. They'll never let this go so easily.

After a few more slow drinks, and Jolene keeping her promise not to talk, I'm ready to go. From the look of Jolene, she's ready to go too. Her gorgeous eyes look tired and are surrounded by dark circles. The red lipstick she wore in the beginning of the night is now pink and uneven on her pouty lips.

"You ready?" I ask her, as if this has just been a normal night for old friends.

"Yep." She slides off the bar stool and takes her bag from the hook on the counter. She pulls out her phone and starts typing something. Glancing over for a brief moment, I see she's on a car service app.

"Are you calling a car?"

"Yeah."

"Why didn't you drive?"

"After not remembering how I got home the other night, I figured it was more responsible not to drive myself. I've seen so many tragedies in the ER from drunk driving accidents. I don't want to be one of them."

"Cancel that. I'll just drive you home."

"I don't think that's a good idea."

"I didn't ask your opinion on the fact that I'm driving you home. Now cancel that and let's go."

"Do you usually drive home from the bar after a night of drinking?"
Why the hell is she so nosy?

"No. I have friends that will give me a ride. But thanks to you, I'm completely within the legal limit to drive tonight. Want to know my shoe size too?"

Jo rolls her eyes, but I swear she wants to laugh. Even though Finn gets pissed when I pay for my drinks, I still leave money sitting on the bar every time. I place a hundred under both of our empty glasses, then follow her to the door. Daphne's eyes may as well be burning a hole straight through me while her devil grin makes me shake my head. That girl is something else. Now I have to figure out how to explain this to her so she doesn't think it's something it most certainly isn't.

———

The silence I had wished upon us while sitting at the bar is now piercing my ears as I sit across from her in the living room I had sworn I would never be in again. It's hard to ignore how smooth her legs look as she crosses them then straightens her dress to cover her knee. Her dark hair is still perfectly curled and laying against the front of her shoulder. It was Jolene's eyes that drew me to her the first time we met. The contrast of her light golden eyes and her almost black hair had me from the get-go. I've gained a bit of restraint with each passing year, but if I'm not careful, she could easily pull me in those. The clock on the wall ticks with each second that passes without a word spoken. I can't believe I let her talk me into coming into this place. Again.

"Jolene, I—"

Her head hangs and her voice is low as she cuts me off. "I know it's been a long time. So much has happened. You know I have a hard time being honest. As much as I hate being that weak woman, some days, I just need someone to sit next to me. I just need to not be alone. Most of my friends were mutual with my ex. Not one of them called me after the divorce. I just wanted to get out of my own head and this godforsaken house. Even if it was just for a few hours. Even if it was just with you."

A deep fire rises inside of me. I want to put my arms around her and tell her everything will be fine. Her ex must have done a number on her. Seeing how badly she's hurt makes me want to track him down myself. But then I would have to admit that I feel something for Jolene, which I'm not sure how that would even be possible. Not to mention, I did the same fucking thing.

"Sometimes things happen that change your life. But it doesn't have the same effect on anyone else around you. They don't know why you've changed and tell you to move on and leave the past in the past. Like the past wasn't just yesterday. You can rip the Band-Aid off but the scar is still staring you in the face every day as a reminder. It's not weak to not want to be alone. It's human."

A tear streaks down her rounded cheek, and she flicks her finger across it quickly in an attempt to hide it. I wish she was better at that. She is the most beautiful crier I have ever seen. The water pools in the bottom of her lashes, creating a river of gold from the reflection. Her bottom lip, which is slightly larger than the top, tightens.

"I'll be fine. I just need a break from my everyday monotonous life every now and again."

"You will be fine, Jolene. I know it."

Jolene grins and does that thing I always loved. She bows her head slightly, smiles with a closed mouth, and a blush comes across her cheeks. I've got to go home before I do something that I shouldn't. I rise from the chair and hear the clicks of Jolene's high heels behind me as we walk through the living room. She kicks them onto the mat as we reach the front door. She loses about an inch of height and I smile. She holds the door open as I walk out, and when I'm halfway down the stairs, I turn to her.

"See you Wednesday?"

Her shoulders drop in what looks like relief. She barely nods.

"See you Wednesday," she says.

I watch until Jolene's front door is completely closed before I pull out of the parking space in front of her house. It isn't until I'm a block away that my blood turns cold and my palms get clammy against the steering wheel. *What the fuck did I just do?*

Chapter
Four

—

Jolene

My mother's criticism is usually endless. When I went to medical school I didn't go to the right school. Then I didn't move to the right town. Then I didn't accept the right job. Now I don't want that job anymore and I'm wrong for not wanting it. It's a never-ending battle with her. I know she loves me and that's why she wants the best of the best for me. But it's also the reason I've always been more of a daddy's girl.

"No. I haven't gone back to work yet, Mom."

I can hear the disappointment through the phone. Her loud sigh shows her age. She used to argue with me until I was just physically unable to argue any further. My mother should have been a lawyer. She could have won every case. But it seems as the years have passed, Mom has been giving in to more disagreements than she ever used to. That doesn't mean she doesn't try to change my decisions, she just doesn't drag out the argument for as long as she used to.

"Jolene, you have a career that called to you. You know death unfortunately comes with it sometimes. You are a nurse, not God."

Called to me? Forced on me would be a better way of putting it.

"I don't want to talk about this anymore."

"Good, me neither," she says, sounding bored. "How's the dating app going for you?"

Completely annoyed and not wanting to give her any more ammo than she already has, I ignore the question. I should have never told her I was using that app in the first place. "Where's Daddy?"

"Out playing golf. I swear he would live on the 18th hole if they let him."

The short laughter shared between us is genuine but heavy.

"Well, I suggest you hurry up and fix yourself, otherwise you won't have a job for very long. Then where will you be? You don't have anyone else to count on anymore." Mom takes a deep breath in and slowly lets it out. "I want what's best for you."

"Thanks for the reminder that Luke isn't here anymore. I needed that," I say sarcastically. "You want what you think is best for me? Or what makes me happy?"

"In order to get happy, you need stability. Strength. Work ethic. You don't get those things by hiding in that house and ditching out on your responsibility."

"I have to go, the timer is going off to pull out my egg casserole. Tell Daddy to call me."

"All right, dear. I love you."

"I love you too, Mom."

That conversation went easier than I thought it would minus the divorce jab. For the last three weeks, I've been dreading every phone call from my parents. Both of them think that I'm on some kind of leave from my nursing job in the emergency room at the hospital. I didn't tell them that I actually quit and have no plans on ever going back. Dad isn't happy about said fake leave, but he's a bit more understanding about it than Mom is. Losing a patient is the hardest part of our jobs. I just wasn't prepared for it to be this hard. I wasn't prepared to lose a patient while they were holding my hand and begging me to save them right before they slipped away. Not sure anything can prepare you for that.

The ceramic coffee cup burns my hand as I gaze over the elongated table in my parents' dining room. My mind is filled with pictures of Paul in his sleek dark suit leaned up against the wrought-iron railing. It's been a week since Paul invited me back to O'Reilly's. After the night we had, where I practically forced him to sit next to me in the pub, it's hard not to believe that the only reason he asked me back is because he feels sorry for me. Even still, I'd love to get the hell out of this house. The last couple of weeks have been making me absolutely crazy.

My phone dings with a message from the dating app I was using. I've only given one person a chance at a date, and after he stood me up, I've had my fill already. I wasn't even sure I wanted to go on that date. Carter has still been messaging me both through the app and on my regular text messages. Every time, apologizing for not making our date at O'Reilly's. It was sheer stupidity that drove me to giving him my phone number, so I know that if don't answer his message on the app, he'll just text me next. I've been out of the dating game for so long. Hell, I'm not even really sure I ever was technically in the dating game. I met Luke right after I graduated high school. These are uncharted waters. So, like an idiot, one night I just gave him my number. I keep telling him not to worry about it, but he doesn't seem to be getting the hint. I'm overly annoyed with the situation. I need to delete this app, not just because of Carter, but because I'm not ready. Just as my finger is about to hit that shaking X to delete it, I get a text message.

> **BILLIE:** *Okay, I've let you have the time to yourself you wanted. But if I don't see you soon, I may go absolutely crazy. Do you want to be responsible for that? I miss your face. Want to meet for lunch? Say, Friday around one at Figi's?*

Billie was the only reason I went into work every day after my divorce. When things got too real, she was always the one to go to for a laugh. She was also the first person to hold me when I lost my first patient. She's by far one of my best friends but I always feel guilty putting my issues out there.

> **JOLENE:** *It's so good to hear from you. Yes, Friday at Figi's sounds perfect. I miss you too. Can't wait!*

Now that I have something else to look forward to, it makes the decision to stay home tonight much easier. I'm a far cry from a woman with her shit together. Paul was probably caught off guard and asked me to come knowing that I probably wouldn't anyway. Besides, the danger that got me in so much trouble years ago is still shining brightly in his eyes. I need to stay far away from Paul, and that's exactly what I plan on doing.

———

Gasping, I sit up straight in bed and pull the sheets up to my face.
BANG BANG BANG
The knocking on the door gets louder with each round. Even the creaks in the hardwood floor freak me out as I sprint into my parents' bedroom, which faces the front of the house. Through the white sheer curtains, I see Paul's dark sedan in front of the house just before Paul steps back and looks up to the window. My racing heart pounds against the hand that I've placed over it to stop it from fully exiting my body. *I'm going to kill him.* Heading down the stairs, I try to calm myself, but steam could be coming out of ears I'm so mad. With the click of the lock and a creak of the door, Paul stands in all his sexy, hazardous glory on my stoop.

"What the hell are you doing here, Paul? You scared me senseless." My voice is a whisper and a yell all in one.

"You didn't show up."

"What?"

"It's Wednesday. You said you were coming. Then you didn't." Paul's face is emotionless, though his booming voice has plenty of emotion for me to know he's pissed.

"I didn't think you really wanted me there, anyway."

"Did I ask you to come?"

"Well, yeah."

"Then I wanted you there." The tension is making even the outdoor air feel thick and heavy. "You don't tell someone you are coming and then just don't show up. Makes the mind wander. Don't like it." Paul looks down to his suit jacket and straightens it by the lapels. It's obvious he's trying to hide how bothered he is, but surprisingly, he's not doing a great job of that. I've just about had it with everyone and their opinions and feelings lately. Carter tried to make me feel bad for not going out on another date with him, and now Paul is getting on my case about not showing up to O'Reilly's. A growl comes from within me as my hands flail out to my sides, then slam onto my hips in frustration.

"Well, allow me to free your mind. I won't be joining you at O'Reilly's again. I thanked you for bringing me home and that should have been the end of it. I was just trying to make a point when I showed up last week. I didn't have any plans on ever seeing you again. You may be able to intimidate other women into doing what you want, but you have no idea the kind of woman you're talking to. So you can take your anger and shove it."

The strength I feel from standing my ground is liberating. Even in high school, he had that smooth deep voice that commanded you to him naturally. He could have talked me into just about anything back then. But just because his voice is hypnotic doesn't mean that I'm under any spell he's casting. He's overreacting anyway. It wasn't a date. For crying out loud, we aren't even really friends. As I'm dripping with pride for resisting the Paul charm, I realize he isn't responding how I thought he would. Instead of nodding his head and walking back to his car, he stands in front of me, eyes burning. His front teeth bite his lower lip. His eyes are glazed and staring. And not at my face. Knowing exactly what he's looking at, I close my eyes and tilt my head back as I internally scream obscenities. Of course I would be standing here in my silky, short, black night dress. The cool air has put my nipples at full alert and goosebumps have taken over my legs.

Paul takes a slow step toward me, his tongue now licking the part of his lip that his teeth just scraped across. I take one back. But it's too late. He's already crossed the threshold into the house and, without taking his eyes off of me, he softly closes the door behind him. The intoxicating flicker in his eyes can make me do just about anything as long as he touches me. This is the Paul I remember. The one I needed to forget.

"Damn, you've only gotten sweeter with time."

"Seems you've only gotten more dangerous."

A smirk crosses his face, and his hands remain in his pockets as he saunters the extra step to me. He smells of cinnamon and mahogany.

"I guess that depends who you ask."

I watch his lips make every shape as he speaks. Yep. Definitely. Dangerous. I spot the blanket that I draped over the couch earlier in the evening and launch myself at it. His eyes move back up to my face as the blanket covers my mostly exposed body and I increase the space between us. I'd be lying to myself if I denied that Paul isn't having an effect on me. Just his scent alone makes me want to rub all over him like a teenage girl on prom night.

"You should go." I'm not telling him he needs to leave for his own sake. I'm saying it for mine.

"Want me to go?"

"Probably for the best."

One of his eyebrows raises. "That's not what I asked." Paul again closes the distance I had placed between us. "Do...you...want...me..."

My lips burn as they press heavily against his as a need so deep rises to the surface. A touch of warmth that I haven't felt in so long and didn't want from anyone else. His tongue slips past my lips, moving with intent inside. The goosebumps return as the blanket drops to the floor, but warmth comes back to my body as Paul's large hands move quickly over my naked arms. The kiss deepens as his grip lands on either side of my head and my body moves all the way into his. My legs begin to cramp. I've been standing on my tiptoes to reach his kiss for too long. I lose his lips as I go flat footed but only for a second before he leans down, places his hands on the back of my thighs, and picks me up. My legs impulsively wrap around his waist, and a hiss releases as I feel his erection against me.

The heat of the moment pauses as I realize we've moved to the bottom of the stairs. The stairs that lead...upstairs. The bedrooms are up there. I pull back from the embrace I don't want to let go of and look at him. There's doubt in his eyes. I can see it.

"Maybe we should..." I begin.

Paul immediately releases me, and we separate a few steps from each other. He's completely calm and put together. I can only imagine how I look. Hair a fucking mess. Lips red from the pressure of his, and I can't for the life of me seem to catch my breath. We both stand in front of the other, staring into the other's eyes as if they are going to tell our stories without words. I'm not sure many people could spot the anguish that lies deep behind those brown eyes. But I can see it.

"Sorry. I shouldn't have kissed you like that."

"I shouldn't have kissed you back. You're just so…damn."

"I'm just not ready for…," I admit still trying to gather my bearings.

"Neither am I."

I feel the heat rise up to my cheeks and a smile hits my face. Then my heart practically stops beating in my chest as he smiles widely back at me. My heart beats in my ears with every step he takes toward the front door. My body, angry with the loss of his touch, moves forward a step before I stop again. Paul sees my movement forward and turns back to me. His eyes match mine in what seems like an unspoken agreement that tonight will be a one-time deal. One time to let loose and feel pleasure with someone I know. It's been so long. His hands reach out for me and I lunge at him. Any hesitation is now obliterated from the intense pull. Paul lifts me with his hands on my ass, and I wrap my legs around him once more. Hands in hair. Lips over skin. Steps taken two at a time. I feel a turn to the right instead of to the left.

"My room is that one," I pant and point in the opposite direction.

"I know where your room is, Fancy."

"Oh God, you're not…"

I lose my ability to protest his direction as his mouth encloses around the lobe of my ear. Fingertips grip tighter onto my back as the cool sensation of his tongue slips down my jaw. The room darkens, and I know where we are. Just as I'm about to say something, Paul rocks his erection against my clit, and all sense of right and wrong vanishes like a puff a smoke in the wind. He tosses me onto the bed in my parents' old room. My eyes close, and my cares leave as his hand trails from my ankle to my knee and up to the hem of my underwear. His thumb pauses briefly and rubs back and forth over my hip bone before continuing up both sides, raising my night dress. My breasts release from the fabric, and his wet lips enclose over one nipple sending electric currents through me. His hands raise the dress over my head while his tongue does circles around my breast. My hips begin movement on their own from the need surging within them. The force of his hand behind my neck pushes my head up and toward his eyes as his lips begin a slow descent.

Not wanting to be the only one giving something for the eye to see, I sit up and push off his jacket. He straightens allowing me access to the buttons on his shirt. Two get undone before my antsy fingers have had enough of the buttons and pull the shirt up. Paul grabs it from me and pulls it up over his head. I thought I knew Paul. I think a lot of people think they know Paul. But the secrets he carries hang like weights under his suit jacket. Including what he's been hiding under these swanky suits. Every place on his body that gets covered by a shirt is covered in tattoos. My fingertips sprawl over his chest and feel all the way down to his stomach. When you look at Paul, he doesn't look like he would be as ripped as he is. Each muscle is hidden until it tenses under my touch and they come out to play.

I press my lips to his stomach while unfastening his pants. His hand wraps under my chin and he angles my face toward his. My eyes flick up just in time to see him leaning down to connect our lips again, and his pants fall to the floor. His arm curls around my back, and he scoots my body further onto the bed. Our movements becoming quicker and more intense. The tip of his erection spreads me gently as he teases my clit with each circle of his hips. The friction lessons as my slick arousal causes him to slip easily over my opening. His heat leaves my body briefly, and I hear the tearing of the packaging. Desperate to feel some part of him, my leg brushes back and forth against his until he returns to me.

"Jolene." His eyes roam over my face before coming back to mine. Unlike earlier, I'm picking up on the vibe he's giving off. I don't know what the hell I'm doing either. But it feels good and right in this moment. That's enough for me. I pull his face down to mine and thread my fingers through my hair as my lips take his. My leg wraps around his waist, pushing his body into mine. A sharp inhale raises my breasts into his chest as he enters me.

"Oh fuck, Jo," he moans.

Our bodies move together in desperate need. It doesn't take long for me to begin feeling that tingle that starts deep in the pit of my stomach. Paul devours me, delving deeper and deeper as my breathing picks up. My grip on his arms tightens and one arm moves down. Suddenly the pad of his thumb circles the spot that makes me completely come undone. His relentless thrusts through my orgasm increase the volume of my moans in the room. I open my eyes to see the god above me. His tongue slides across his bottom lip just before his teeth clench together as he hisses through his climax. His movements slow before he removes himself and collapses on the bed next to me.

Clearly, I must be out of shape because I'm huffing as if I've just run four miles. He takes one deep breath and is breathing normally. With my senses rushing back into my brain, my eyes widen when I realize what just happened.

"Oh my God. What the hell did we do?"

"Please tell me you're fucking joking right now. I didn't push you into anything."

"I'm not talking about the sex. No, I wanted that. But not in here." A deep guttural laugh comes from Paul. "It's not funny. Do you have any idea how uncomfortable this is? I just had sex in the bed my parents used to sleep in."

Paul shoots off of the bed and pulls my arm to help me off of the bed. He gathers our clothes off the floor and leads me into my room on the other side of the hall. He drops the clothes on my floor, then leaves me to go to the bathroom. While he's gone, I can't help but think how weird it feels that he knows his way around this house. It's been so long. We were just kids. Well, maybe I was just a kid. Paul was always much wiser than his years. He had to be. There were responsibilities he had that most his age never even knew of. Life wasn't easy for Paul back then, and from the look in his eye earlier, it doesn't seem like it's easy now either.

"Hey, you okay?" Paul's voice pulls me out of my thoughts. I hadn't heard him come out of the bathroom. Didn't see him either. I was sitting on the edge of my bed staring at the floor.

"Yeah. I'm good."

I watch as Paul pulls on his pants, then he comes to me and squats at my feet.

"You have those dimples in your forehead. What are you worried about?"

Dimples? I rub my forehead to get rid of whatever big mouth dimples are there.

"Nothing. I'm totally fine."

He touches his hand to my cheek, then pushes up from his squat and places a gentle kiss on my lips.

"I have to go. But don't think I'm running out to be an ass. My phone is going to go bat shit crazy in about two hours. I need to gather myself before then. I'll call you tomorrow."

I nod, then squeeze the hand he placed into mine and give him another kiss. Paul grabs my feet, twists my body, and places them on the bed. The warmth covers me as he pulls the comforter up to my shoulders. He smiles at me, then turns to throw on his button-up shirt and grab the rest of his things. Just before he walks out of my room, he turns back to me.

"I'll see you when I see you?"

I nod. "See you when I see you."

The look that crosses his face as his tongue slips out of his mouth to lick his lips says a lot. He winks at me, then the sound of his footsteps disappears down the stairs, and I hear the door open and close. Paul was nothing but trouble back then, and he's nothing but trouble now. But damn did trouble feel good on me.

Chapter
Five

—

Paul

"I'm fine. I swear. Everything is straightened out with Mr. Edinbaugh, and the meeting is rescheduled for tomorrow."

Never in my entire time of being in the business with Benson have I ever missed a meeting due to my own negligence.

"Don't know if I believe you. I mean, Edinbaugh will get over it. I'm not worried about that. But I know something is up with you. Spill it, or I find out myself."

"Knoxx you don't have the stamina to outsmart me when it comes to that shit. Don't even try it, or I will do nothing but laugh in your face when you find nothing."

Benson laughs on the other end of the phone. If he weren't over three hours away and on a new job site for a house he's building on the side of a mountain, he'd be all up in my business. Benson is my best friend, but I'm glad there's a little distance between us now.

"Anything else, boss?" I ask jokingly.

"Are you ever going to give that up? You own half the fucking company."

"Sure thing…boss."

"You're such an ass. Talk to you later."

Benson hangs up and I breathe a sigh of relief. There was a slight chance that Benson was going to try to dig deep. Daphne was working at the bar last night. She noticed that not only did I not drink, I left early too. Once she blabs that to Sophie, I'm going to have that nonsense to deal with.

I fill my coffee cup, and the day feels completely off. Calls start coming in around seven in the morning. I'm usually already in the office, yet here it is almost eleven and I haven't even put on pants yet. My hip leans against the counter as I let the first sip singe the front of my lip a bit as I blow lightly on the hot liquid in the cup. I would have been fine if I wouldn't have had that dream again. An hour power nap would have taken care of me for the day. I used to get less growing up. But I was so deep into this nightmare I not only slept through my alarm but through every call I got. Not a whole lot scares me. Not anymore. I've seen so much turmoil and crime. Heartache. Robberies. Murder. But this recurring nightmare is something I can't shake easily. It doesn't have blood or any of those horrible things I've seen in the past. It has one woman. She's at the end of a road and no matter how fast or hard I run, she never gets any closer. The white dress that covers her body blows in the wind. Suddenly she turns around and there's no face. It haunts me. I know exactly who that nightmare is about and it's a daily reminder of what is gone and will never come back. The milestones in my life that I just won't have. And I deserve that for not being able to save Heather. For giving up on her.

Most of my work today is all on my computer, so I call my assistant, Tina, and let her know that I'll be working from home today. I spend ten minutes convincing her that it was really me on the phone and that I'm not having a mental breakdown. I haven't missed a day in the office since I took over the main helm at Knoxx Developments. Even on the weekends, I'm there. So Tina's concern doesn't surprise me.

With the chill of that nightmare still fresh, it will be difficult to concentrate on the contracts I have to look over today. I finish the last few drops of coffee, toss the cup into the sink, and head to the bedroom to get ready for the gym. That should do it.

—

Walking into the gym in the middle of the day is making me feel like a kid at a new school. At night, there's hardly anyone in here and I don't have to worry about potentially seeing clients or those who want to talk my ear off. I come into the gym to blow off the anger. The pain I put myself through is nothing compared to the feeling of walking around this town every day.

"You all right?" a familiar voice comes from behind me as I continue my reps. I don't need to look up to know who is standing behind me. Finn always comes during the day, but I didn't expect to run into him today.

"Yeah. Why wouldn't I be?"

"The five-foot-two brunette."

The loud clanking of the chrome steel dumbbells being placed back into their nest says everything about my frustration.

"Nothing to do with her."

"You can't bullshit me. I got eyes and I know what I saw. On more than one occasion."

Finn slowly walks behind me to the shoulder press. I know he isn't going to let this go. Maybe the only way to get him off my back is to just spill what happened.

"Look. We dated in high school. We kept in touch a little bit along the way, but it'd been a long time since I've seen or heard from her. So when I saw her in the pub, it was a shock, that's all."

"All I'm sayin' is that it's been three weeks since she walked into that pub and you haven't had a Wednesday binge since. You might be able to deny something's going on, but I can tell there is."

Nobody knows me better than Benson. We stood right next to each other through every shitty detail of our lives. Every happy milestone, too. But Finn is right behind him. We may not have the history together, but Finn knows almost everything.

"There's nothing going on," I tell him.

"Then why did you miss a meeting this morning? Not to mention, you're spending part of your work day at the gym."

My eyes roll toward the ceiling as a deep annoyance takes over.

"I can see you and Benson have been talking. You know I'm a grown fucking man, right? I don't need the two of you watching over my every move. In all of these years, I've never called off sick, or overslept, or canceled a meeting. I'm fuckin' human, so get off my ass."

I get off of the machine and walk back to the lockers. Apparently, this isn't the place that's going to help me today. I don't even bother changing. I grab my bag and head out to my car. The engine roars to life, but instead of backing out and heading back home, I sit in silence. I've never snapped on Finn before and I'm feeling bad for doing it. The passenger door opens and Finn gets in.

"I ain't tryin' to be on your ass or make you feel guilty about nothin'. But I notice when shit feels off, and lately, it's been way off. I know you're attracted to that girl and I know it's fuckin' with your mindset. But eventually you gotta…"

"Gotta what, Finn?" My voice is low and whispered. "Move on? Take a chance? I couldn't save her, man. I was sitting in jail while Heather died in that alley. I broke her heart, and then she died. I'm incapable of sustaining love and I've come to terms with that. Now all of you are going to have to do the same."

Finn moves his hand across the stubble on his face. He looks at me as if he wants to say something but doesn't. Instead, he smacks his hand on my shoulder, gives it a squeeze, and then gets out of my car.

Jolene's right. I'm dangerous. I hurt everyone that cares about me without even trying. I've gotten used to living my life alone. I'm not easily defeated. I try to keep my head high, my brain busy, and my body moving. But today, for the first time in a long time, I feel pretty damn defeated.

Chapter
Six

—

Jolene

"Thank God it's Friday," Billie says. "That hospital is a madhouse and getting worse by the day."

"That's no surprise to me. I've always thought working in the emergency room was a madhouse. It also doesn't make me miss working there one bit."

I've had a bad feeling about that job from the day I accepted it. Quitting was the best thing I could have done for myself. Although, now I'm desperate to find something new so that I can get the hell out of my parents' house and get a place of my own.

"So what are your plans? Have you been looking for another job or just taking some time?"

"I've applied at a few places, but there's one I'm really hoping for. Something a little more my speed. A small family practice."

When I decided to go into nursing, I had every intention of looking for a position in a doctor's office. If my father hadn't intervened, my life could've been completely different. He was so excited to have his daughter working for the same hospital as him. My father loves me, and I know that he was trying to do right by me, but truth is, I felt guilty that

I didn't want the job and took it just to appease him.

Billie clears her throat and my stomach plummets as her eyebrows furrow. Her cheery smile turns down. I know exactly what she's thinking.

"Billie…" I warn. My palms begin to clam up and I can feel the intense beating of my chest. Just thinking about it brings me back to that day on the floor in the ER. The day that Billie is referring to. The day I knew I could never go back to that hospital again.

"How are you really doing? That day was tough for all of us, but I can't imagine how you—"

"I don't really want to talk about this." I slather butter all over the bread the waitress set on the table and take a huge bite.

"Did you call the number I gave you?"

Shaking my head, I just shove more bread in so that I don't have to tell her how I threw the number away. I couldn't call the crisis line. I didn't want to explain to them that I'm a nurse working in the ER and I can't handle death. I want to pretend that day never happened. She sighs, and then shoves a piece into her mouth too.

My phone starts ringing from my bag. Normally, I'd ignore any phone calls while having lunch with Billie. But with my pending applications, I have to answer it.

"Hello?" My voice comes out higher than I intend.

Billie snickers and whispers, "Too eager."

"Hey…uhhh… hey, Jolene. You've been ignoring my texts so I figured I would call you." Hearing Carter's voice on the line for the first time shocks me. Now I'm regretting accepting the call. "I was hoping you would give me another shot and go out with me tomorrow night."

"Oh…uhm… I'm sorry, but…" *Think, Jolene, think.* "I'm seeing someone."

Billie's eyes light up and she clinks her wine glass against her plate on accident as she tries to set it down on the table. *Oh shit.* I'm so involved with Billie's reaction that I don't realize that Carter hung up. "Okay, bye," I say to no one on the other end of the line and then return my phone to my handbag.

I take a long drink from my water glass. "So," I ask Billie, "what's new with Samuel?"

"Oh. I don't think so, girl. Back up. Who is this guy and why am I just now hearing about him?"

"No, it's not what you…"

Billie sighs loudly, "Damn I was just going to set you up with one of Samuel's friends for the Heart Gala."

"What?" The thought of going on a blind date actually terrifies me. Even worse when I would be stuck with him at the gala with no escape. "Sorry. Taken." A nervous giggle comes out of my mouth as I try to quickly shove the Caesar salad that was just placed in front of me into my mouth.

"I'm so glad. I was worried you would feel a little uncomfortable at the gala going alone. I can't wait to meet him." The loud clank from my fork hitting my plate as I begin coughing from nearly choking on a crouton makes Billie jump. "You okay?"

"Fine. I'm fine."

Shit. I would do anything to not go to that gala at all. Maybe I'll fake a sickness. The flu? Food poisoning? The plague?

"Don't you even think about ditching out on the gala, Jolene. I know you too damn well, and I will come drag your ass there myself if I have to."

Billie's husband Sam is one of the event co-chairs. She hates going just as much as the next person. But she doesn't have a choice and, for the last few years, I haven't had one either. I should tell Billie the truth about my fake boyfriend. She would understand why I just told a lie. But it's been a long time since I didn't see pity in Billie's eyes when she looks at me. Every time I looked at her all I saw was that "how are you holdin' up" looking back at me. So she thinks I have a little boyfriend. Big deal.

"I guess now would be the time to tell you that Luke will be there." *Oh no. She said his name.* "Word is, he put a ring on that twenty-five-year-old's finger."

The blood in my veins goes stagnant. Any romantic feelings that I had toward Luke are gone, but that doesn't stop the slice of pain that sears through me at the mention of his name. Or that he proposed to the woman he started seeing two weeks after he told me he didn't love me anymore. Our divorce was finalized a year ago and I haven't seen him since. I'd give just about anything to make it stay that way.

"Maybe I won't be making the gala this year."

"Don't you dare!" Billie's stern voice matches the look on her face. Like a child, I pretend to throw a fit in my chair and Billie laughs. "Great. Now what are you going to wear?"

"We'll have to go shopping," I say.

Billie squeals in excitement. I wish I could match her sentiments.

Lunch with Billie felt better than I thought it would. For too long, I've allowed myself to sink into the sand. Now I have to dig myself out. How am I going to do this now? I can't go to the gala alone. There's no way in hell I'll ever let him know the truth. The truth that he shattered me and I haven't come close to moving on. My dream of a family and white picket fucking fences was blown to smithereens in a one-hour conversation. He doesn't need to know.

All the way through the grocery store, I contemplate what I'm going to do. The gala is in two weeks and I have no dress, let alone a date. It's not until I get next to the frozen peas that I know what I have to do. I cringe at my phone as my finger presses on his name.

"Fancy?" Paul's concerned voice sends a shiver down my arms.

"Don't call me that."

I hear a snicker on the other end, then another voice. He's with someone. *Is it a woman?*

"No. He said the counters were going in today and they are going in today. You tell him I don't give a shit if it takes him until midnight, the counters get put in today. Trust me, he doesn't want to lose our contract." I hear a man respond in the background. "What's up, Jo?"

Relief pulses through me. If I didn't know any better, I would say that could have been a small hint of jealousy. *Crap. I'm in trouble. Abort! Abort!*

"You sound busy, never mind."

"You okay?" Paul's voice has lost any amusement that was there a second ago.

"Uhm. I need some help."

I've always felt that I do a good job at hiding the anxiety when I speak. Paul, however, I have yet to fool.

"Where are you? I'm leaving now." Paul's voice is almost scary and I hear the jingle of car keys on the line. "Where are you?" His booming voice makes me jump.

"No, I'm fine. Everything is fine. I just need…a favor."

"Jesus Christ, Jo. Never start a conversation with 'I need help' unless you are in serious trouble." The breath pushes from his lungs and it sounds like static in the phone as it passes by the speaker. "I'll come to you. Where are you?"

"I'm out running errands right now, and I don't know when I'll be home. So it will be easier for me if I can just stop by your place later on. Unless you'd rather meet at O'Reilly's or something again."

"Nope. Not at O'Reilly's. I'll text you my address and you can come by after seven. Should I have dinner delivered?"

"Dinner?"

"Good grief, Jo. I need to eat. You need to eat. Stop making such a big deal."

This has already gone way farther than I ever thought. We never should have let it get as far as it did the other night. It seemed we both needed to feel like we were still alive. But that is where this ends. Well, other than this favor I need.

"I eat early, so don't worry about me. I'll see you later."

———

Now this is a sight. Standing in front of the address Paul gave me, I can't believe that he lives here. He was always so critical of my parents' fancy lifestyle. Now here he is, living in one of Boston's newest neighborhoods in one of the tallest buildings. The entire bottom level is made of clear glass, showing the lobby, front desk, and concierge. As I approach the large double glass doors, a man in a suit opens it for me while tipping his head. The lobby feels cold. Almost sterile. My wedge heeled shoes echo as I walk slowly through the open space. It's bright even though the light has faded outside. The floors and walls are all made of a white stone with a mix of light and dark gray veining strewn about. Slowly, I keep heading straight until I arrive at the elevators and then make a left turn like Paul instructed. There's a narrow hallway with three elevators on the right and one on the left. My heart beats faster with every echoed step I take. The clear button glows white after I press it. The elevator door opens and, reluctantly, I step inside.

The ascent takes a few minutes. I have no idea what floor I'm even going to because there was only a keypad where I punched in the numerical code from the text message. When the door opens, I'm greeted by a very strange foyer. The cold, white stone scheme from the main lobby is mimicked in the circular room. A white six-panel door is located on the other side of an empty round table that sits in the middle of the space. It's hard to picture Paul living here. Not that there's anything wrong with the design. It just isn't Paul. The door swings open, and I nearly choke on my spit when Paul comes into view. He motions for me to enter with his naked arm that's attached to his naked chest that's attached to his naked stomach. *Mother fu*—

"C'mon in."

His gray sweatpants hang low on his hips, the legs pulled halfway up his calves. His hair is dripping wet and a white towel is draped around his neck. Nervous and not sure how to start this conversation without drool leaking out of my mouth, I walk into his condo and try to remember what an asshole he is. Paul closes the door behind me as I take in the lack of furniture. The open living room is in front of me with the dining room, the kitchen to the left. The walls, floors and cabinets are all white and empty. So is the counter. No coffee maker, no utensils, not even a toaster.

"Did you just move in?" I ask.

"Been here about two years."

Paul watches me walk through his hollow condo to the doors of the balcony. The glass stretches from the ceiling to the floor and takes up the entire wall. Looking out at the reflection of the glowing city in the harbor, I can see why he would like it here. The view is amazing.

"You need a favor?" Paul asks from behind me.

"Right," I say as his voice pulls me from the mesmerizing beauty of the water. It has nothing on the view I have as soon as I turn around though. Paul's leaning against the wall, ankles crossed. He still apparently hasn't found a shirt, and it's getting warm in here. Unlike the lobby and small foyer leading up to his front door, the inside of his condo is dark. The only light comes from a small table lamp that sits on the only end table in the entire space. It gives off a warm hue, almost illuminating his body in a halo of gold. A black leather couch sits against the wall next to the table and faces a mounted flat-screen TV.

"Are you in trouble?"

He squints so briefly that if I wasn't staring at him, I would have never seen it.

"No. I'm not in trouble."

I need to come out with it, but my nerves are silencing my mouth. Even if I had everything together before I got here, it would have fallen to pieces the second he answered that door looking like that. He crosses his arms gently in front of him but low enough for me to make out his chest tattoo that I have never seen before. Two doves sit amongst intricate shading and rose petals. A clock with roman numerals sits in the center of his chest and a skull below it. On one bicep, a compass sits with a world map as a background. The other bicep is covered with trees that look like it makes up a forest. Between the drip of water dangling from the tip of his hair, the tattoos, and the lines on his hips that lead to yet more danger, I can't take my eyes off of him. I don't even notice that I've been practically chewing on my finger. *Jesus! Snap out of it, Jolene.*

"I kind of need you to... Oh God." My hand hits my head, and I sit down on the couch. This is going to be so humiliating.

"Spit it out, Jo."

I take a deep breath. "So this guy has been messaging me nonstop from a dating app that I signed up for a few months ago. He called today for the first time while I was having lunch with a friend, and I kind of told him I was seeing somebody just so he would stop messaging me."

"So what's the problem? You lied to get the fucker to back off."

"My friend got all excited, and before I could explain to her that I was lying, she went crazy and wants to meet said guy."

"Ohhhhhh. I know where this is going." Paul smiles, but it isn't a good smile. It's devious. Sinful. "You may as well just go ahead and ask me. Let me guess, double date?"

Irritation suddenly builds, as his arrogance is pouring out of him. I stand and begin marching toward the door. My hand barely brushes the handle before he pushes in front of me.

"I'll do it. On one condition."

"Oh, here we go." My eyes roll and I can only imagine what is about to come out of his mouth.

"Straighten up."

"Excuse me?"

"I've never known you to let anyone dull that gold in your eyes. Stop it. Stop sulking. Stop moping about. He ain't worth it. Get your gold back, Jo."

He walks away leaving his eyes locked with mine until he passes me. With my jaw stuck shut and the threat of tears in my eyes, I try to find my words. My only hope is to pretend he didn't just say that and go on with asking him.

"It's more than a double date. I uh…I need you to go to the Heart Gala with me. Black tie."

"No way. I'd go meet her, do a double date. But a gala? Not my thing. I do everything in my power to stay the hell away from large groups of people outside of work."

The fact that I'm going to have to go alone hits me. I'm going to have to tell Billie the truth. I'm going to have to face Luke alone. In a fit of panic, I blurt out the first thing I can think of to get out of eye sight to gather myself.

"Can I use your bathroom?"

His eyebrows furrow and I can't blame him for being confused. The question came out of my mouth louder than we had been talking. Nerves do that shit to me.

"It's down the hall, second door on the right." He points in the direction of the bathroom, and I can't run there fast enough. There must be something seriously wrong with me. It's not just the fact that Paul doesn't want to pretend to be my boyfriend for a night, it's that now I'm a big liar too. Once in the bathroom, I look at my reflection in the mirror. I tuck my hair neatly behind my ear and straighten the front of my blouse. How pathetic I must look to him. Maybe on the way home tonight, I'll find a nice big hole to crawl into.

After a few minutes of pretending to use the bathroom, I walk to the couch where I set my purse down, but it's not there. Instead it's hung across the room, neatly over Paul's coat on the only hook by the front door. I've never known him to be so concerned with being tidy.

"Is that the only reason?" he suddenly asks me from the kitchen. "Is the only reason you are so upset about going because of your friend?"

Damn it, I hate how well he can read me.

"Luke is going to be there."

"I see."

"With his new fiancée."

"Ah. Now it all makes sense. You don't want him to see you there, alone. Tell me. Why do you care?"

"He said I was boring. He said I lacked adventure. Our life was too routine for him. He was right."

"So you feel the need to prove yourself to a guy who doesn't matter anymore?"

"It's fine. Don't worry about it. I just won't go." My cup of embarrassment is overflowing at this point, and I'd rather just give up and disappoint Billie than beg this man for anything. I begin to walk past him when his hand firmly presses against my stomach, stopping my movement.

"The hell you won't. We're going. He'll hate me. It'll be so entertaining."

A wicked smile crosses his face and a giggle escapes me. His eyes widen for only a second as if he were a lion getting a better look at the lioness before ravishing her.

"I better go," I say quickly and head to the door.

He matches me step for step out of his eerily empty house and around the odd table in the foyer. Before getting into the elevator, I turn back to him.

"Why don't you have anything in your home?" The words come out softly. I was reluctant to ask. He doesn't speak as the elevator opens and I step in. Just before the doors close, the pain on his face is unmistakable.

"I just sleep here. Homes are for families."

Chapter
Seven

—

Paul

The muscles in my arm burn like fire as they stretch and pull, but I still don't come close to touching her. Every time I get closer, she moves further away. Her white dress flowing in the wind that steals my breath away. Her long hair blowing behind her. "Come back," I yell. Her head turns and my eyes sink into a black abyss that shatters my heart.

The pain shocks me awake to the sun's reflection in my mirror. With shaking hands, I rip off the sheets and covers that have been covered in sweat. "Motherfucker." I grit my teeth together. I can't escape it. Even in my dreams, I'm the piece of shit that fails her. So cruel. My phone begins its daily explosion and, just like all the other days, I do my best to brush it off but know it will continue to haunt me all day. Every day. My only hope is that I become numb.

The entire ride to the office is a blur. I hit the lock on my key fob and my horn echoes in the parking garage. That beep reminds me about those text messages I saw on Jolene's phone last night. It was going off repeatedly for over a minute. I thought maybe there was an emergency or something, so I checked the phone. I shouldn't have. I have no right to be looking at her phone. But the texts just kept coming. There were way too many from whoever this Carter is and he is persistent. He doesn't seem to be taking the fact that she is seeing someone lightly. A twinge. That's all I need to feel to know this guy is bad news. I bet it will only take Everest a half an hour tops to tell me everything I want to know about him.

"Whaddaya need?" Everest's deep voice on the other end makes me smile. He's the one that sat by my side the night I found out Heather died. He didn't say anything. He didn't try to give me a bro hug. He never even said the classic 'I'm so sorry for your loss.' He gave me the best advice I've ever heard. 'Love will take you down faster than any bullet. You cry tonight. Tomorrow, you bury that shit.'

"Need you to look someone up for me. I'll text you the only info I have: a name and a phone number. You got the time?"

"You know I got the time. Send me what you got. Give me an hour."

The call ends before I step foot into the office building. It takes me a second to realize that the reason my coffee isn't waiting for me on Tina's desk is because it's Saturday. Unless something big is going on, my assistant doesn't work on the weekends. In fact, the place is empty compared to a weekday. My adrenaline kicks in when I see my office door is cracked open when it should be closed and locked. The door swings open with a tap of my foot and, seeing his brown briefcase on the chair, I already know who's here and looking out over the harbor.

"You're late."

"You're such an asshole," I tease, making my way across my office. Benson stands up from my desk chair and wraps his arm around me. "What the hell are you doing in town?"

"Sophie wanted the kids to spend some time with Finn and Daphne. School's on spring break, so it was a good week to come. My foreman is handling the project we're working on right now, so here we are. Thought maybe you could use some time off."

"No. Absolutely not." Ignoring Benson and his ridiculous assumption, I walk around him and grab the contract I'm supposed to be going over this morning.

"Figured that would be your response. What can I do? Put me to work."

"Aren't you here for family time off?" I ask.

"You know me. Just like you, I need shit to do."

Part of me misses working with Benson. We've been friends for so long that it just comes naturally. But that also means he knows when something is bothering me and it's obvious he's already noticed.

"I'm sure there's some filing that needs to be done."

"I almost forgot how funny you are," he says, then takes one of the contracts off the desk and begins going over it.

As we work throughout the day, I know it's coming. As the clock gets closer to dinner time, I can feel the air becoming thicker. Benson sits in the chair opposite of me, puts his feet up on the desk, and leans back with his fingers laced together on his stomach. I straighten my papers, then tilt the chair back and stare right back at him.

"Who's the girl?" Benson asks, breaking the silence in the room.

"What girl?"

"Like I don't know? It went down in Finn's bar for fuck sakes. You know Daphne tells Sophie whenever someone sneezes. I know all about how you went beast mode on some dude for having his arm around whoever this girl is. I also know you don't do that shit for just anyone."

I don't want to tell Benson. The minute her name comes out of my mouth, assumptions are going to be flying rampant. I also know that if I don't tell him, he'll go find out for himself.

"Jolene," I say quietly.

"Jolene? As in Jo, Jolene?" Benson can barely contain his excitement. He's not even really trying to hide it.

"Yes."

"Ho-ly shit."

"I know what you're thinking, but stop it. It's not like that. She was drunk and some guy was trying to take her out of the pub like that. I couldn't just watch that shit happen."

"Oh." A small piece of the excitement leaves Benson's face. "No, you wouldn't. But I thought Daphne said that she came in again after that?"

Immediately, I begin straightening the papers that I already straightened. I stand up from my desk and grab the suit jacket that was draped across the back of the chair. "Yeah, she did."

"She also said that the two of you left together." Benson smiles, and from the look on his face, he can tell something happened.

"What is this? A goddamned beauty parlor? He said, she said bullshit? Get out of here."

"Paul," Benson says, his tone now serious. "Paul." Benson places his hand on my shoulder. I know what he's going to say and I wish he wouldn't say it. He's said it to me before, and every time he does, it's the only time that hate him.

"She'd want you to be happy."

I pull my shoulder away fast, tossing his hand off of it. "I was. Twice. Then people decided I was a piece of shit and made me lose everything."

"I never said that. Don't you put words in my mouth, Paul. That never came out of my mouth."

"It didn't need to. 'Stop dating my sister' was enough."

Without giving him another look, I walk out of the office. The conversation with Benson put the cap on the type of day I was already having. It couldn't get much worse. Then I get a text back from Everest.

> **EVEREST:** *No listing. No address. No matching name. I'll be digging on this one.*

Now, that's not what I expected to hear. I know what this means and it's not good. I don't know who this guy is, but until we find out, I'm going to have to keep a close eye on Jo. My gut is telling me something is far from right. I exit out of the text from Everest and pull up Jo's last text to respond.

> **PAUL:** *Busy tomorrow night? Was thinking we could meet up for dinner to go over some details of this arrangement.*

Immediately I see the three little dots dancing indicating that she's typing back. A strange feeling happens deep in my gut. I don't know why. This is just business.

> **JOLENE:** *Yeah, I can do that. Where do you want to meet?*

PAUL: *Be ready at five. I'll pick you up.*

———

Jolene seems nervous sitting across the table from me at Amadeo's. Her wine glass emptied within the first five minutes of sitting down.

"I've never been here before," she says.

"Really? This is Benson's favorite place in the city. If Sophie would let him, he'd order food from here every night. That's kind of how I got addicted to it."

The waiter appears at the table to take our order. I'm mesmerized by Jo's smooth skin as her lips move. The noise that once took over the room is nothing but a buzz as I watch her smile sweetly at the waiter. The perfection that sits across the table paralyzes me, and all I can think about is grazing her neck with my tongue.

"Paul?" The sound of her voice brings the noise from the restaurant back, and I realize that both she and the waiter are staring at me. "Are you okay? Do you know what you want?"

Quickly, I turn to the waiter and say, "I'll have the same."

The waiter nods and leaves the two of us at the table.

"When is the gala?" I ask.

"Saturday."

"We need to have a plan. A story. Like how we met and how long we've been dating. Those are the two most common questions people ask when you introduce them to your significant other."

Jo takes a long drink from her fresh glass of wine that the waiter brought when he came to take our order. From the way she's downing that wine, I would say she doesn't want to do this any more than I do.

"Well. We were high-school sweethearts."

Something sinks in my stomach. That's true. We were.

"We went our separate ways after high school and then ran into each other in a bar one night." She smiles looking proud of herself. "We might actually get through the night without really lying a whole lot."

I nod. "Just keep it simple. Nobody needs details. They all just want one thing. To hear a magical fairytale so that they can continue to lie to themselves that they actually exist. Nobody gets a fairytale."

"God, you're cynical," she scoffs.

"Think about it, Jo. Picture a present wrapped in the most beautiful wrapping paper that you've ever seen. But inside is a pile of shit. Just because it looks beautiful on the outside doesn't change that it's just a box of shit. You may think people have these perfect lives. Truth is, no one does."

The smirk on my face at my brilliant analogy has no effect on her expression. She stares at me with blank eyes.

"What the hell happened to you? You used to be so…"

"We aren't going there. I used to be young and dumb."

"No. You used to be full of fire. A volcano."

"I'm going to this gala. That will be an adventure," I laugh.

"Tell me what happened. What girl broke your heart so badly that it turned you into this cold stone?"

Before I could stop myself, I blurted, "She didn't break my heart. I broke hers."

Jo lowers her eyes from mine to her twiddling fingers. I know what she's thinking. I broke hers too. I don't want this conversation to turn badly, so I give her what she wants to know.

"I broke up with her. We were fighting. She died before I could make it right. End of story."

As her golden eyes return to mine, filled with pity and sorrow, I can barely stand it. I have to change the subject, or I'm getting the fuck out of here.

"So what's your favorite drink?" Her face twists in confusion. "If I have to go get you a drink, I'd like to know what I have to order."

"Oh. Right," she says. "Vodka and cranberry juice. Whatever you do, no shots. I'll be wasted two in."

"Oh, I think I've already witnessed that and, I have to say, it's not pretty."

"Thanks a lot," she laughs. "Not my proudest moment."

Jo's phone begins beeping from her bag. She ignores it.

"Do you need to get that?" I ask her.

"No. I'll check it later."

"Go ahead. Answer it," I push.

"I already know who it is. I'll get back to them later."

I already know who it is too. I'd be willing to bet it was the same person who was texting her twelve times in one minute the other night.

"Got to tell you something. Don't be pissed," I say.

Jo slouches back in the booth and her eyes roll back into her head. "Oh God. Usually when someone says that, it's never good."

"I looked at your phone when you were in the bathroom at my place."

"Yep. Pretty mad. And what is your reasoning behind looking at it?"

"It was going off. Constantly. Thought maybe there was an emergency. Didn't want you to miss it if it was. But then I saw all of them were from some asshole named Carter. Is that the guy who started this entire mess?"

"So now I'm a mess. This is going really well, Paul. We should get together again soon."

"You know what I mean. Is he the guy from the dating app?" She nods. "Give me the phone."

"No," she squeals.

"C'mon. Just give me the phone. I'll end this shit right now."

"I can handle it."

The phone beeps again, and the anger builds within me. If he won't quit messaging for her, he will for me. "Just give me the goddamn phone, Fancy."

She growls at me, but hands me the phone anyway. I press on his name and lift the phone to my ear. Jo's eyes get wide when she realizes I'm calling him.

"Paul, don't. Hang up," she demands.

I hear the line pick up and a deep voice say, "Hello." Oh, this is going to be so therapeutic. I clear my throat and smile.

"You call or text my girlfriend one more time and they'll be selling pieces of you down at the fish market."

Calmly I press END before anything else can be said and hold the phone over the table. Only Jo doesn't take it. She looks frozen in place and her face has gone pale. All I can do is laugh. She finally snaps out of it as I wave her phone in front of her face for her to take it.

"I can't believe you just did that. You can't go around throwing empty threats at people."

"Who says its empty?" Her eyes widen. "Let me know if he calls or texts you again." I say. The waiter places our food on the table. I dig into my steak right away, and surprisingly, it's cooked perfectly. I had no idea what I was even getting. "You ordered well." Jo ignores me, and it takes her some time to get over being mad. Soon she sits back up straight and eats.

"Whether you like it or not, Jolene, people suck. Sometimes, you just can't be nice. Now c'mon, eat up."

After a while, Jolene begins loosening up again and laughter begins to flood our table as we reminisce about our past. Like the time she was trying to sneak out of her house to come meet up with me but fell into the bushes instead and woke up her parents. She never even made it past the sidewalk. I keep the stories of our past coming, just so I can hear her laugh. Something about that sound draws me into a stupor, like a witch casting a spell on me. I watch the lines of her face change, her head tilt back and her perfect white teeth shine behind her usual red lip. The later it gets, the more I want to bite that pretty red lip. Time to get her home before we make the same mistake twice.

—

It's not easy to keep my eyes from looking at her smooth thigh peeking out from the slit in her casual dress. The blue interior lights in my car highlight her skin, making it impossible to ignore. We pull up to her house long before I'm ready to let her out. It's an odd feeling that I haven't had in a long time. Then again, I haven't had too many friends that I hang out with anymore. Benson and Finn are like brothers, and Sophie and Daphne are like sisters. It's just not the same.

"Thanks for dinner," she says, smiling.

"What are you wearing to the gala?"

"I'm not sure. I'm going shopping with Billie tomorrow night after she gets off work. What color are you thinking?"

"I don't wear colors. Black suit. White button up. No tie."

"Well, I guess that will be easy to match." She opens the car door and gets out.

"I'll wait until you get inside."

She nods and begins to shut the door, but hesitates. "I'm glad you were in O'Reilly's that night. You were always saving me."

A lump forms in the back of my throat. She has no idea how badly I wanted to be the one to always save her. To love her.

"Red."

"What?" she asks.

"If you want him to hate himself, wear red."

She nods with a huge grin, shuts the door, and I watch her until the door to her house closes. Not only will her ex hate himself for letting her go, I'm making it worse on myself. Jolene never deserved the life her father planned out for her. Always putting himself and his feelings first. She deserves to be put first, and if this is what she needs, then I'm going to give it to her. Then maybe I'll be able to live with the fact that I fucked this up for us.

As I pull away and the lights of passing cars shine in my eyes, I can't stop thinking about that man's voice on Jolene's phone tonight. I know there's something going on with that guy. She's in trouble, I can feel it. My hands turn clammy and my breath quickens as the memories of Heather return. What if I can't save her? I pushed Heather into danger. I didn't save her from it, and it killed her. Jolene needs me to follow through on this gala date, but once that night is over, so is all of this. I can't be trusted with her. And even though I've only known the feeling of numbed vacancy in my chest for years, a harsh ache sits heavy.

Chapter
Eight

—

Jolene

"**Y**ou have got to be kidding me," I shout at the coffee maker that just broke and spilled water all over the counter and floor. It broke once before, but I was able to fix it and get it running again. Without coffee, my patience is nonexistent, so I pick up the machine, walk outside in my camisole and pajama pants, and throw it in the trash can. Ever since I quit my job, it's been easy to sleep in late. It's almost noon. I haven't heard anything from Carter in two days. Paul must have really scared him off the other night. I throw on the first pair of stretchy leggings I can find with a tunic top and head to the coffee shop with my laptop.

The first sip of morning coffee is always the best one you'll have all day. I can only imagine it's like being in a desert and that first sip of water confirms you are going to live. The place is busy, but I find a little table by the window, and I open my computer to load up. As the cup gets closer to my lips, my eyes close as I brace for the blissful moment.

"Hi there."

Caught off guard, I jump and spill the hot coffee all over my lap.

"Ouch! Hot! Holy hell that's hot!"

"Oh my God! I'm so sorry!" The familiar woman begins grabbing all the napkins she can get her hands on and helps pat me dry. "I didn't mean to startle you. Shit."

"It's okay," I lie. The top of my legs feel like they are still burning. But I don't want her to feel bad.

"I'm Daphne. I work at O'Reilly's. I'm friends with Paul."

"Right." I smile through the pain. "I knew I recognized you. I'm Jolene."

"I know....err...Nice to meet you, Jolene."

What the hell did that mean? She was quick to change what she was about to say, but I caught the part where she already knew my name. I can assume that Paul has been talking to her about me.

"Want to join me?" I ask as I point to the other chair at my table.

"Oh, I don't want to ruin your morning any more than I already did."

"No. It's fine, really. If you were planning on sitting down in here, it would be weird now for you to sit across the room."

Daphne laughs and nods in agreement. "What was that?" she asks, pointing at my mostly empty cup.

"Hazelnut blend. But you don't have to get me another one. I can get it."

"No way. I made you spill it. Be right back."

She places her coffee on the other side of the table and then goes back up to the counter. Now that she's going to be sitting with me, I don't want to be rude and be on my computer. I close my laptop and place it off to the side. Through the window, the leaves blow on the spring flowers that are popping up all over the city. It's a serene moment before my phone beeps.

"I guess it didn't work," I say to myself while I forcefully swipe the notification of Carter's text message off of my phone.

"Everything okay?" Daphne asks as she places my coffee cup in front of me and then sits down.

"Oh yeah. No worries. So you're a friend of Paul's?"

"We're really close. Safe to say we're like family. My husband, Finn, is one of Paul's best friends. I own O'Reilly's with him and his brother."

"That makes sense why you already knew my name then."

Daphne's face scrunches playfully. "I don't know too much, actually. I know your name and that you two are old friends. Everything else I've gathered myself."

"What do you mean?"

Daphne takes a drink from her cup and she looks around the room. She's hesitating, but I can tell she wants to say something she shouldn't. She places the cup back on the table and begins tracing the top rim with her finger. She watches the movement of her hand, but even without seeing her entire face, the emotion is heavy in her voice.

"For a long time, Paul just looked like an empty corpse walking around. It was like he was a machine just going through the motions of everyday life. Looking at him was like looking into a black hole. I worry about him. Within the last few weeks, I can actually see the color of his eyes. You're having an effect on him."

Heat rises up into my cheeks, and I can only assume that they are the color I usually wear on my lips. "And apparently…he's having one on you." Daphne smiles. "I came to give you a friendly warning that he's a broken man. But I think from the look on your face just now, that isn't necessary."

"We're just friends. He's doing me a favor, and then we'll probably go our separate ways again."

Just friends. I think I'll leave out the fact that we slept together in a heated fit of desire. Probably also a good thing to leave out that every time he sucks in that bottom lip I wish he was putting that mouth to good use instead of keeping it all to himself.

"I see. Well, Paul did mention that you're kind of on your own here lately. So I wanted to let you know you're more than welcome to come hang out with me in the pub. The only nights that Paul comes in are on Wednesdays."

The curiosity peaks inside, and I want more information about who Paul is now.

"Why only Wednesdays?"

"Girl, like I've said, Paul is like a brother to me. He knows just about everything there is to know about me. He doesn't like to admit it, but he had a part in saving my life once. And after all of that, he won't even tell me what the hell his deal is with Wednesdays. All I know is, they aren't good for whatever reason, he usually ends up drunk, and Finn brings him home."

I'm even more curious about his routine weekly visit to the drinking hole. Daphne and I sit together for a while, talking about fashion. Her bouffant blond hair and AC/DC shirt paired with black skinny jeans make her look like a badass. My emerald green silk tunic matched with black leggings and ballet flats couldn't be more opposite. I love her style, but it would never look as good on me as it does on her. It's easy to see why Paul is so fond of Daphne. She's easy to talk to.

"You should come hang out with me this week sometime. I work mostly in the evenings until close, so come anytime. Drinks are on me," she says as we pick up our things from the table and throw away our empty cups.

"I might just do that."

"Well, I've got to get to work. Hope I'll see you soon."

"I'm sure you will."

That came out so quickly from my mouth, and I know how she interpreted it the second I look at her face.

"I'm sure I will."

—

"That's an obscene number of dresses, Billie."

Billie has always been good at spending her money. But she's really good at spending someone else's money. I've been shopping with her before, and every time I do, I always spend more money than if I would have just gone myself.

"Oh c'mon. This is the best part. Any excuse for a new swanky dress."

My parents were very strict on my clothing choices when I was growing up. Probably why I always leaned toward a more polished look. It used to be a lot of fun getting new dresses and going to the opera or ballet. We did it often, and maybe that's why it has lost its appeal for me anymore. Billie, on the other hand, has more dresses than she can carry draped across her forearm.

"You better be trying some of those on, too."

"I already got my dress," she laughs.

After trying on the eighth dress, I don't know which one to pick. Billie has such great taste, and I can't decide between a few of them.

"I like this one," I tell Billie as I step out of the dressing room to show her. Her eyes roll.

"Of course you do, it's the most boring one I chose."

"It's simple, sophisticated, and elegant," I say.

"It's boring, drab, and makes you look old."

My mouth hangs open as I take in a large gasp of air. "I resent that," I yell, laughing, and throw one of the empty hangers from the fitting room at her.

"Put on the black and red one," she hollers.

"I don't want to."

"Why not?"

"Because there's no back and half of the front is missing."

"You can totally pull that dress off. Put it on."

I stare at the dress for a few minutes as it hangs in front of me. It's a beautiful dress, but I'm just not sure it's for me. I look back to the dress I just took off that Billie said was boring. It's a classic professional-looking black dress that would be comfortable and I wouldn't have to keep checking to see if all my bits and pieces were still inside of it all night. Staring at the red flowers that cover the black lace material has my nerves bouncing. It's so far out of my comfort zone. Suddenly, I hear Luke's voice in my head. "*I just think we've gotten too comfortable. I need more adventure. More spice.*" I'll show you spice. I practically rip the dress from the hanger and pull it over my head. The fabric clings to my skin as if it were made for me. The deep V cut in the front reaches to my lower sternum, showing a small amount of the sides of my breasts. Then I turn to see my entire back open to the air. The dress dips low in a matching V all the way down to just above my rear end. I don't know how someone would wear any underwear at all with it. As much as I wish I was in my early twenties, that decade is long gone and it took my perky tits with it. Billie jumps up from the bench outside of the fitting room as I exit with my hand covering half of my exposed bra in the front.

"Put your damn hand down and let me see it." She pushes my hand out of the way and gives me an evil grin.

"It's a beautiful dress. It's just…"

"It's just going to make him regret every decision he's ever made. This is the dress."

As I look in the long mirror at the end of the dressing room, I remember what Paul said. And it is one of the most gorgeous dresses I've seen.

"Fine. This is it. Does that mean I don't have to try on the other five dresses you have in there?"

"Yep. All done."

My mood instantly improves knowing we can get the hell out of here. I grab my phone and take a small picture of the material, not revealing any of the details of what the dress actually looks like.

JOLENE: *Red.*

I send the text along with the picture of the fabric to Paul. It's not until after I hit send that I find myself second guessing sending it. Then I find myself watching the phone awaiting his reply. Snapping out of it, I toss my phone back into my bag and finish changing.

Billie and I are standing at the counter checking out when I get a weird feeling. The feeling like someone is watching me. I've felt this way once before, and even though it was a long time ago, I remember exactly how I felt. I quickly scan the store, but nothing seems out of the ordinary. Then I see a man standing back by the fitting rooms and he's staring at me. His gray scruffy beard is being rubbed with his hand as if he's trying to think. My hand reaches for Billie's arm as he pushes himself off of the wall and walks toward us. Billie turns to see the man and she moves closer to me.

"Are you Jolene Barrington? Dwight's daughter?"

"Yes." I'm reluctant to answer, but I feel like I've seen him before.

"I thought so. Wow. You've grown up, haven't you? I haven't seen Dwight since the last golf tournament we did together. You tell your old man that Winston says to call him."

"Oh, of course. Winston, it's nice to see you again. I'll make sure to tell my father to give you a call."

He flashes a kind smile, then walks back to the fitting room just as his wife comes out. Relief takes over and Billie tugs her arm out of my grasp.

"You okay?" she asks.

"I saw him walking toward me and I couldn't place him. That's all."

"Ready?" She grabs my dress from the lady behind the counter. I nod and walk quickly to the door. Just as the cool air hits my face, my phone goes off.

PAUL: *I thought you were raised with better manners than to tease a man with a picture.*

Paul's text message makes me laugh out loud, and Billie stops in the middle of the sidewalk. I ignore her and text him back. For some reason, it didn't occur to me that sending him the picture of a small portion of the dress would be a flirty move. But with his response, it's almost too easy.

JOLENE: *Wait until you see the whole dress. Or lack thereof.*

I giggle and look up to see Billie giving me a look.

"I've never seen you so happy. I can't wait to meet him."

Oh God. Change the subject. *Think Jo, think.*

"Want to grab a drink? I know a good place."

"I haven't been out for a drink in months. Let's do this."

I know that Daphne was heading into work and I haven't spent time in any other bar lately. I nod and take her to O'Reilly's.

It isn't until we walk into the front door that I get nervous about being in Paul's territory. But that feeling is fleeting as Daphne spots me and begins waving her arms in my direction.

"Hey! Glad to see you took me up on my offer."

"It just worked out tonight. This is my friend, Billie. Billie, this is

Daphne."

Daphne reaches over the bar and shakes Billie's hand. "What can I get you two?"

"Vodka and cranberry," I say right away, and Billie orders the same.

Soon there's three glasses in front of both of us, and the three of us are having a great time. Every time Daphne gets a free minute, she comes over and chats with us. We're all laughing and tossing back drinks when the smell of spice takes over my nose and the temperature rises at my back.

"What the hell is going on here?" Paul's voice comes from behind me. My head spins around, and I watch him take the stool next to me.

"What are you doing here? It's not Wednesday," Daphne asks, eyeing him up and down with a suspicious look on her face.

"I got a distracting text message today, and ever since, I just couldn't concentrate. So I thought I'd take the rest of the night off."

Daphne's brows are drawn to the center of her face as she stares at him for a second.

"That's weird. What the hell kind of text message would..." Daphne takes a glance in my direction, and I must have guilty written on my forehead. "Never mind. What do you want?"

"Whiskey. Reach high." He smiles, and a small wrinkle curves around his tilted lip.

The fluttering in my stomach needs to calm the hell down. But I can't help it. He looks damn good. His black button-up shirt is only buttoned three quarters of the way up, revealing a small portion of the ink that hides underneath. His sleeves are rolled up, revealing the indentations of his muscular forearms. Shockingly, he isn't in dress pants but jeans that look perfectly made just for his body. He may as well be on the end of a popsicle stick because I bet every woman in this bar would lick that shit right up. Once I can get my vision unstuck from him, I remember that Billie is sitting right next to me. And from the look on her face, there is no going back and telling her the truth now.

"Billie," I whisper, giving her a slight elbow bump. "Wipe the drool off your lip." Billie's mouth hangs open in full swoon.

"Don't tell me you're Paul?" she asks, not believing that this could be the man I was telling her about. The man that is supposedly mine.

"Okay. I won't tell you," he says, giving her a smile that is only worsening the situation.

Her nervous giggle makes Daphne and I begin laughing. Paul rises from his stool.

"I'll be right back." He gently taps the bar, then walks to the back of the pub.

"Damn. You should be at home with that and not out here wasting all your time with me," Billie jokes. I just let that joke go and suck back the rest of the liquor that's left in my glass.

"Do you want another?" Daphne asks.

"Absolutely."

She nods, and I wonder how much she actually knows about Paul and me. It seems like the entire bar turns their heads to watch Paul walk out of the office and back into the bar. He may as well have been walking in slow motion. Returning to the stool next to me, I watch his lips slowly part and, through the glass, watch the amber liquid flow in. The night he had those lips on me begins to flash like a strobe light in my mind. The heat begins to build down low in my core. I've got to get myself under control. We're just friends. Just. Friends.

Chapter
Nine

—

Paul

It's not my usual routine. I rescheduled my appointment for this evening after I received the image of that damn dress on my phone. I've had a hard time getting Jolene out of my mind. Every night before bed, I see her. A repeat of the night I showed up at her house and saw her in that next-to-nothing silk dress she had on. It's almost as if I can feel her fingertips against my torso as she unbuttoned my pants. But then, I'm assaulted with the images of her young, damaged face as I broke her heart on the front stoop of her parents' house. A breakup that wasn't my idea nor something I wanted. But that didn't matter. My heart has only loved twice. Leaving Jolene broke it. When Heather died, it got buried. There's been many days that I wish we could backtrack. There's just so many things I would have done differently.

I've got to keep it straight with Jo. She doesn't need me polluting her world again. But then her vanilla perfume infuses the car and clouds my thoughts and judgment. After she and Billie were done with their drinks, I offered to take Jo home. I glance in her direction only to see her already looking at me.

"Thank you."

"For what?"

"All of this. I've felt alone for a long time and now I don't. Even though this relationship isn't real, and I don't even know if you want this friendship, it just feels nice to know someone has my back for once."

"I'll always have your back, Fancy."

Tonight, I saw Jo in the most raw form I may have ever seen her. While sitting next to her, feeling trapped in this constant hell, she looked so free. Unlike her, I felt like I was in a prison with only a window to look out at something I could have had but I lost my chance. I tried to ignore it and make it look like I was enjoying the night. I guess some part of me really was. Being next to her, breathing in her goodness, makes me feel like I could be good. It always did. Maybe that's why I was so in love with her all those years ago. When all my trouble began, I wanted to be good for her like she was good for me. I wasn't. I'm still not. And even knowing all of that, I still don't want to let her go. I want to grab her face and kiss her. Hold her. Take away all the pain that anyone has ever caused her. The pain that I've caused her. But she's still the girl too good for me. And I'm still just the boy from the wrong side of the tracks.

I can feel Jo's eyes on me as I shut the car off and get out. She opens the passenger door and gets out before I make it all the way to her side. I match her step as we make our way to her front door. I should have stayed in the car and just waited for her to close herself inside of the house. When Jo doesn't reach for her house keys right away, I know that I've made a mistake. She turns to me, her gold eyes tormenting me.

"Billie likes you," she giggles.

"Looks like you and Daphne hit it off pretty good."

"We did. She wants me to hang out with her and Sophie Friday night."

I nod nervously. I'm glad that she'll have friends like Sophie and Daphne. They are a few of the best people I've ever known. But then there's the reality that she's going to be hanging around friends that I hang around. Some ground rules need to be set to keep things from getting out of hand fast.

"You'll have fun. But I think we need to be very clear on what is going on here."

She knowingly nods in agreement.

"We're friends." Her hands begin to fumble with the straps on her purse.

"Exactly," I say, knowing what I'm feeling is so much more.

She tilts her body toward mine, and her touch upon my chest is all it takes. Any control I've had up until this point disappears. My arms wrap around her small waist and my fingertips press into the curves. Our lips meet—only this time, it's not like it was before. She presses her hips into me, and her tongue breaks through my lips. With a little scrape of her nails on the back of my neck, I deepen the kiss and pull her closer if that's even possible. Jo's mouth pulls away as her head tilts back, giving me the space I needed to run my lips down her jaw.

"Paul," she whispers through her moan, and my body stills.

My vision focuses and I realize what is happening. Slowly, I pull myself back and reluctantly let her go.

"I better leave. I have an important meeting early in the morning."

"Of course," she says quickly. The disappointment in her eyes takes my breath. I want it gone. Now.

"I'll call you tomorrow?"

And just like that, it's gone, and that happy girl I love to see shines bright again.

"Yes."

Not wanting to leave without feeling her once more, I lean in and kiss her cheek. As I back away, a rosy blush takes her cheeks. Once inside the car, I look to see her wave from inside, and in that exact moment, something hits me hard in the chest. A beat. A real, heavy, beat.

—

"Hey, Tina." I grab the coffee from her desk that she had gotten me. It wasn't her job to get me coffee. I've never asked for it. But Tina is one in a million and she's been with this company for years. Benson and I have always ensured that she is well taken care of and, in return, she does the same for us. So every day she buys me a coffee when she buys hers. "Just send in my first appointment whenever he arrives."

"Will do," she says. "You look different this morning. You okay?"

"Yes, of course."

I rush into my office before Tina can ask any more questions or make any assumptions. The leather gives a deep squeak as I lower myself into my chair. With a slight push of my foot, I spin around to the wall of windows that overlook the harbor. That feeling of blood rushing around in the cavity that for so much of my life was completely empty has only increased since last night. Maybe I'm not dead inside. *Maybe…*

A knock on my office door interrupts my thoughts. I'm looking forward to keeping busy today. Hopefully, time passes quickly.

"Come in."

I rise from the chair and make my way around the desk to greet my next potential client. I examine the front of my suit as I fasten the middle button on my jacket. These meetings were difficult when I first began the take over of the city division. Trying to have others believe in me when I was so unsure of every decision I was making didn't come easy. Apparently, I was good at faking it. Now, they almost bore me. So, I take a deep breath and blow it out silently as footsteps enter my office. Only this is no potential client. The man that stands before me is not one I wanted to step toe to toe with again. Yet here he is.

"What are you doing here?" I move back to my chair behind the desk.

"I think we need to have a little chat."

I bet he does. He walks past me, further into my office, as I close the door behind him. His eyes are on me as I take a seat behind my dark oak desk. I fold my hands and sit patiently, waiting for him to speak. I have nothing to say.

"Why are you back? How did you find her again? I thought we had come to an agreement." Jolene's dad takes a seat in the chair on the other side of my desk. His casual demeanor as he is toying with his daughter's personal life is disturbing, yet not surprising.

"Seems we have different definitions of agreement."

"I find out that she's quit her job at the hospital and has been lying to me about it. Imagine my surprise when I then find you kissing my daughter. I have a hard time believing that her life falling apart at the same time I find you with her is not a coincidence. You were supposed to disappear. Forever." Dwight's face is red, indicative of his elevated blood pressure. He hated me before he even met me. He heard my name and that was enough for him. Never even gave me a chance.

"She's an adult now. She can make her own decisions."

"You think so? She went from being a successful married woman, to a divorcee and unemployed. And here you are." Dwight takes a breath and then brushes lint off his dress pants. "Stay the fuck away from my daughter. Or you won't like what happens next. You ruined her back then, and you're ruining her now. We had an agreement. You owe me for what I did for you."

"What you did for me?" My voice raises as I rise from my chair. My hands slam onto the surface and my body leans across. It's the only thing between us that is stopping me from laying him out right here. "You blackmailed me into breaking your daughter's heart. What kind of a father does that?"

"A good one. The kind that knows a criminal doesn't belong with his daughter."

"You know damn well I didn't do it."

"Yeah? Well, a few counts of larceny on your record and spending a year in jail says otherwise."

He's trying to bait me and I know it. Back then, when my entire world was falling apart right in front of my eyes, I would have taken him down in a heartbeat. But now, there's something to lose.

"We aren't kids anymore and you don't hold the power you once did. If you don't get your sorry ass out of my office, I'll have you removed."

Removed would be the most humane response I could give at this point. It's taking a lot of willpower not to strangle him. I'd love to watch as his eyes get wide and his skin turns blue.

"You don't leave my daughter alone now, you'll regret it. And so will your delinquent mother."

"Time's up." With my patience dwindled to nothing, my shaking hand slams onto the phone receiver, picking it up.

He quickly stands from the chair. "Just because you work in an elaborate office, doesn't change the fact that you are never going to be good enough for my daughter. Any piece of trash can put on a suit."

"Get the fuck out."

Every muscle in my body shakes with adrenaline as he smirks then turns his back to me. I never wanted to kill someone more than I did in this very moment. If it wasn't for Jolene and her love for her father, that man wouldn't have walked out of this office. It's going to take a lot more than empty threats from daddy this time to keep me away. For the first time in my adult life, there's something happening in my chest.

Sophie walks in just as I throw my coffee cup across the room.

"What the hell?"

Barely able to talk through my anger, my finger points to the door. "Dwight fucking Barrington."

Sophie's face turns rampant. "That was him?"

Before I can even finish a full nod of my head, she was out the door and walking toward the elevator. I run out after her. That girl has bigger balls than most of the men I know. She doesn't know everything about my past, but she knows all about who Dwight is and what he did.

"Sophie, don't."

"And why not? He ruined your damn life, Paul. Why are you still protecting him?"

"It doesn't matter. It's my problem. Leave it."

Slowly it becomes clear that Sophie and I are shouting in front of Tina's desk. She's sitting with her head down, but I can see her biting her lip. She looks worried.

"It's okay, Tina."

I nod my head toward my office, and Sophie immediately agrees and follows me back into my office. But once we both get inside and the door closes, she doesn't stop pushing.

"He took everything from you. Who knows where you would have ended up had he not forced you away. He deserves more than what he's getting."

Sophie's face is red and heated. I've only seen Sophie angry a few times before, but Finn didn't give her the nickname of Firecracker for no reason. She is feisty as hell and her mama bear nature only increased after she had babies of her own.

"Just drop it."

"Give me one good reason, Paul. Why aren't you telling him to go to hell and kicking his ass all over this office?"

My frustration of the situation has hit a high, and my hand smacks against my desk. "Because I love her," I blurt.

Right after those words come out of my mouth, silence takes over the room. I don't even know where that came from. I'm not sure I even realized I felt it until the words made it real. Her eyes are wide as she looks over every inch of the desk, trying to avoid eye contact with me until she can't help it anymore.

"I knew it," she says, trying hard to hide the slight grin.

"That makes one of us," I say quietly. "I had no idea I was capable of that again."

"Maybe you never actually lost it. How do you know you haven't loved her this entire time, but those feelings were just buried by grief and guilt?"

My cell phone lights up, and five text messages come in one right after the other. All of them from Jolene.

> **JOLENE:** *Paul. Answer your phone.*
> **JOLENE:** *My father has lost his mind.*
> **JOLENE:** *Incoming!*
> **JOLENE:** *I'm on my way.*

"Shit. She's coming to the office."

"Oh good," Sophie says as she tucks her feet underneath of her in the chair, getting herself more comfortable.

"You aren't staying."

"Oh come on, Paul. You always take away all of my fun. I want to see her face when you tell her the truth."

"Get, before I call the boss on you and tell him you're harassing me at work."

She laughs and pretends to pout while slinging her purse over her shoulder and standing from the chair. Sophie has a way of pulling shit out of me. Things I don't really want to tell anyone. Then she has this magical way of making me feel human afterward. She moves close to me and I know she's about to say something profound. Something I'm going to end up thinking about all night.

"Don't push people away who fight to be in your life. Those are the ones who will fight for you when you can't. Trust me."

As Sophie walks out, I know that she's speaking from experience. She and Benson didn't have it so easy in the beginning, and now look at where they are. But their circumstances are completely different too. I call Tina from my office phone to inform her that Jolene will be coming and to let her straight into the office. As if I could concentrate on any of the black ink on the paper, I attempt to go over a proposal. It doesn't take long before the office door swings open and Jo marches through.

"What did he say to you?"

She stops in the center of my office, throws her purse to the ground, and plants her hands on her hips. One thing that Jo was never lacking was attitude. She was just very careful of who she let see that side of her. I want to be as mad as she is right now. But seeing her after coming to the realization of how I really feel, she just looks so damn beautiful when she's this upset. Her cheeks are flushed. Those big eyes that usually look so wary are narrowed, and her usual pouty lips are pursed up tight. She doesn't even realize that the top button on her V-shaped white blouse is undone and revealing the cleavage below. The black skirt clings tightly to her thighs and ends just above her knee.

"What the hell are you smiling about? Did my father come in here?"

"Yep," I say calmly, my eyes unwavering. I should stay sitting so that my arousal is hidden. But as she walks closer, demanding answers, my body does what it wants. It moves out of the chair and around the desk, closer to her.

"What did he say to you? He came home yesterday to surprise me and saw us kissing on the stoop. We had a huge fight, and the things he..."

"It's all true. Every word of it is true. And you know it. There's no argument to be had."

"You shut your mouth. I'm tired of you saying you aren't good enough. Damn it, look at what you have accomplished. You are so much more than you have ever given yourself credit for. Stop letting my father…"

Against everything I've vowed to myself over the last few weeks, my mouth encloses around hers. Silence takes over the room that was just filled with her furious rant as her tense shoulders fall loose. Her hand lifts, and her fingers push through my hair as she pulls me further into her. Without breaking from her kiss, I walk her slowly back to the office door where I flick the lock. My arm swings around the lowest part of her back, and I pick her up just enough so that her feet aren't touching the floor.

She softly moans into my ear from my erection rubbing against her, and I want more. We reach the desk, and my arm slides all of the papers to one side. Just seeing her ass on the edge of the desk is enough to make me want to break all the rules. The friction between our clothes and our bodies increases the movement of my hips against her. A sound from outside the office door catches Jo's attention.

"Hurry," she begs, and sucks her bottom lip into her mouth.

She grabs the collar of my shirt and pulls my face back into hers as she unfastens the hook to my pants. Her skirt easily pushes up, barely revealing her baby blue lace panties. I'd give anything to make this last. Go slowly and taste every drop of what she's got. But her impulse is as strong as mine and we both know it's the middle of the damn day in my office. In my very busy office. She takes the condom that I fetched from my wallet out of my hand and places it on me frantically. Once in place, her hand begins moving it up and down. The feeling makes my legs weak. I want to slide into her. Feel her readiness for me. I push her panties to the side, and before I can touch her with my fingers, she pulls me closer, guiding my tip into her slick entrance. If the low groan she makes as she feels me pressing into her is the last sound I'll ever hear in this world, I will die a happy man. Those hungry golden eyes peer into mine, telling me she wants it. I push in slowly until I'm buried deep within her. Moving out, she hisses, and I look to the door. The chance of getting caught makes this so much better. I thought that thrill would go away with age. It hasn't. With each slow push and pull, her whimpers grow. It's taking great control for me not to use my voice at all as I feel the ripples and curves from inside of her. Part of me never wants to get caught. I want to stay inside of her for as long as I can. But then there's the other part of me, just hoping someone comes knocking on that door and the adrenaline that would flow seconds later.

I have everything under control—until she pushes one of her heels into my shoulder as she bucks off the desk and the muscles in her legs quake. My hands grip onto her thighs, pulling her body into each thrust, and savoring her climax around me for only moments before my own mind-numbing pressure releases.

"Jesus, Jo," I say, still catching my breath.

I lean down and press my lips against hers before slowly pulling away from her warm core. I grab a tissue and make quick clean-up of myself while she pulls the hem of her skirt back down to her knees. As she buttons her blouse back up and swipes the wrinkles out of it, I notice how dressed up she is.

"Did you get all fancy just for me?"

"You wish," she teases. "I have an interview this afternoon. I was getting ready when I realized my dad had left in a bit of a rage. After our fight last night, I knew exactly where he would have gone."

She looks around my office and her eyebrows furrow. Jolene was always so proper and respectful. The only time she was adventurous was when I would drag it out of her. It's in there, and what just happened on my desk proves it.

"We really should be more responsible. This is your place of business. Not to mention, there's so much between us that's been left unsaid, unresolved…"

Why is it right after sex you start thinking? Maybe it's because your brain gets fuzzy when you start feeling that heat. That yearning for someone so deeply that nothing else matters. Until after. When your brain works again. But, I can't go there right now, and the fact that she is tells me that she has so many doubts. This doesn't feel wrong. This feels every bit of right. But I'm not really the man who should determine the difference.

"What time is your interview?" I interrupt and change the subject.

"Eleven."

"Shit, you're really close to being late. Good luck, Fancy. I don't think you'll need it, though."

She gives me a gentle smile and walks toward the door. With her hand on the knob, she slowly turns back to me, smile gone.

"Paul. My dad..."

"Doesn't matter."

"It does to me. I'm not sure where you and I are going from here. But I'm going to be very clear on one thing. If I ever find out my father's opinion of you had anything to do with you leaving, I'll never forgive him." She takes a small but audible breath in. "Or you. Don't you dare break my heart twice."

With the air sucked out of my lungs, my chest burns. My body flops down into my leather chair. Lifeless. It's as if she cut off circulation to the heart that had just begun to beat again. I love her. So much that I refuse to continue this. I love her so much that I won't break her heart twice. I won't give myself the opportunity.

Chapter
Ten

—

Jolene

Other than the few text messages that we've traded and a phone call, I haven't seen Paul since Wednesday. I've found myself on more than one occasion sitting in my living room and missing him. I was so relieved when Sophie called and invited me for the girls' night out.

"I'm so glad we're doing this. With two kids at home and living in the middle of nowhere eighty percent of the time, I can't even remember the last time I was out on a Friday night." Sophie laughs. "Benson must have noticed my desperation to get out for a bit. He didn't even ask me to watch my drinks tonight."

She tosses back the wine in her glass and smiles wickedly, which makes Daphne and I laugh. Sophie couldn't look like a woman on the loose if she tried. She looks completely put together. Her posture is perfect even for sitting in a booth in a rowdy bar. The baby pink cardigan she's wearing sits neatly against her bright white shirt with a long gold necklace. Her hair is pulled into a low ponytail, showing off her stud diamond earrings that she told me she got as an anniversary gift from Benson. Sitting next to her, Daphne looks like a groupie for an '80s hairband. A really hot groupie. Her sandy blond hair is teased up into a bouffant then pulled into a high pony. Her black shirt has a whiskey logo and a big V cut into the neckline. Her black leather leggings top off the outfit. I'm in one of my favorite green blouses that wraps around and ties on the side with my dark denim jeans. My hair is in a long braid that rests against the front of my shoulder.

"When do you go back to Vermont?" Daphne asks Sophie.

"Sunday." Sophie's face glows as she talks about going back to Vermont. "I love that we have the ability to give our kids the experience of both city and country life. But there's just something about those mountains that will always call me back. The kids seem to prefer it there too. They have much more freedom."

"Just wait until they're teenagers," Daphne laughs. "They'll always want to be in the city then."

"Oh, please don't even make me think about that. Katie gives me enough attitude already. I can't even imagine what it's going to be like when she's a teenager."

I laugh and think about all the hell I put my mother through. And the trouble she didn't even know existed. Like the time I kissed Paul at the farmers market when my mom had her back turned. She had no idea we had been making out every time she inspected a potato or smelled a flower.

"What is that about?" Daphne asks, tipping her chin up at me.

"What is what?" I ask.

"That face. You have one hell of a grin, and I can't help but think it's something good. Spill," Daphne says, giddy.

"I was just remembering how much trouble I got into as a teenager."

"Oh, you and me both," Daphne snips.

"It was mostly Paul's fault," I blurt out.

Daphne and Sophie, almost in unison, take a big drink from their glasses, then both lean in closer.

"My parents had quite the opinion about Paul. My mom and I were at the farmers market. Paul was hiding behind the flower stand. I remember the exact moment he put his hand on my arm and pulled me into his body. He pressed his lips roughly against mine, told me he loved me, then spun me back around just in time for my mother to find me dazed behind her."

Coming out of the memory and focusing back on the two ladies sitting at the table with me, both of them have a wide grin.

"You two should just do it and get it over with," Daphne blurts out, laughing.

"Ew that's gross, Daphne," Sophie says, matching Daphne's laugh. "I don't want to think about Paul and sex."

It gets quiet fast, when they realize that I haven't joined in their laughing. Their eyes get wide as they analyze my face. I can only assume they've caught on. I don't feel uncomfortable with Daphne or Sophie. In fact, it's kind of strange how comfortable I am with them. Like we've been friends for years. The dynamic is natural and easy. That doesn't mean that I wanted to admit the fact that Paul and I have had sex not only once, but twice. Damn my lack of control when it comes to him.

Sophie's face turns serious. "You're really good for him. He's had a really rough go of it. Especially since the wedding."

I shouldn't ask, but the curiosity is overwhelming. "Your wedding? Did something happen?"

She shrugs. "No idea why he got so much worse afterward. Regardless, everything changed in him the day you walked into the pub."

Daphne shakes her head in agreement. "Paul is incredibly loyal and we all know that he loves us. But after that wedding, it was like someone hit the life right out of him. Some days when he comes into the pub, it's downright scary. His eyes would be vacant and black. There were times that he would just stare into his drink as if no one else was around. If you would have asked a few weeks ago if I thought Paul would ever snap out of it, I would have flat out told you no. But now…"

"Now," Sophie interrupts her and clears her throat. "He just seems a little happier."

A look is exchanged between the two, and suddenly, I feel the need to excuse myself for a few minutes. "I'm going to the bathroom. I'll be right back."

It's work to make it through the Friday night crowd to reach the bathroom. Thankfully, it's empty when I walk in and still empty when I walk out of one of the stalls. As I'm washing my hands, the bathroom door swings open and Daphne walks in.

"You okay?" Daphne asks.

"Of course. Why wouldn't I be?"

"Sophie is a worrier, and she was concerned that we said something that made you uncomfortable."

"Not at all."

"Good." Daphne sticks her long fingers into the front of the bouffant and fluffs it up a bit. Then she nods at me and we head back out to the bar. We are barely into the crowd when the atmosphere changes and the hair on my arms stands up. That feeling I had the other night is back. The one where it feels like I have eyes on me. Daphne doesn't notice that I've stopped walking as I begin scanning the bar for anyone possibly looking at me. She's almost all the way back to the booth before she turns back around and comes to me.

"What the hell is wrong? You've gone pale," Daphne says, rushing to my side.

"Oh I'm okay. Just got a weird feeling, but I get those a lot." I flash her a smile, but her face tells me she doesn't know whether she believes me or not. She threads her arm through mine, and we walk together back to the booth.

After our return from the bathroom, the conversation between the three of us gets lighter with talk of Sophie's kids and Daphne's cat. The creepy feeling never really goes away, but I struggle through trying to forget about it. I've been paranoid lately about silly things and I'm sure most of that is because I'm back to sneaking around with Paul behind my father's back. We finish the last of our drinks. The time has passed quickly. Sophie snatches up the bill before Daphne or I can grab it.

"I've got this one," she says. "I've been thinking about doing a barbeque or something at the farm. Do you think you could get Paul to come? He has refused to go back there since the wedding."

The thought of spending time with Paul and the people he considers family, catches me off guard.

"Oh...uhm. I'm not sure. Are you sure I can't give you some money toward that?" I ask, pointing to the bill in Sophie's hand and trying desperately to change the subject. I have no idea what is going to happen after the gala tomorrow night. The gala itself is scary enough. I haven't been able to think about anything else after.

Sophie just shakes her head and leaves cash on the table. The three of us walk out of the bar and toward the parking garage a block down from the bar. We parked on the second floor, and since Sophie isn't a fan of elevators, we decide to just walk up. Our laughs echo off the concrete walls. Then a beep from my phone interrupts us. I see who it's from, and the annoyance is hard to hide. But that annoyance quickly turns to fear. My heart stops beating and my breath quickens as I read the text message from Carter.

CARTER: *New friends?*

Then another

CARTER: *That color green looks amazing on you.*

He's here. He can see me, and this has just reached an entirely new level.

"He's watching us," I whisper in a panic.

"Who is? Who is watching us?" Sophie immediately wraps her arm around my shoulder and pulls me into her while she begins scanning the garage.

"Seriously, Jolene, what the hell is going on?" Daphne asks.

"We need to run."

"What?"

"Run to the car," I say frantically.

The three of us run as the messages keep coming through my phone.

CARTER: *You shouldn't run in those shoes. You might fall.*

My mouth is dry, and it becomes hard to swallow, but we make it to Daphne's car. All of our doors shut, and Daphne hits the locks and starts the car. I have to tell them about Carter.

"There's a guy that keeps texting me. Paul got on the phone with him the other day and threatened him. He stopped all contact until just now. He's describing what I'm wearing."

My words come out quickly and there's no way I could have hidden the fear in them.

"Shit," Daphne says. She throws the car in reverse and peels out of the parking space. Lights shine in the rearview mirror from a car behind us as we speed out of the garage. My initial instinct about Daphne is right. She is a badass. She's driving this car like a professional stunt driver and texting on her phone at the same time. The car is staying on our tail, and I'm still getting messages telling me to pull over now, that I'm putting my friends in danger.

"I just texted Paul," Daphne says.

Sophie replies, "Yep. I got Finn and Benson."

"I should call the police," I say, my voice shaking.

"Paul said not to," Daphne says, looking at her phone then turning to me with a sympathetic look.

Daphne swerves in and out of traffic. My heart beats fast as she hits the gas to blast through a yellow light. Sophie and I both turn around hoping he got caught by the red light, but her worried eyes hit mine when we realize that he's blown right through it. We make a right turn, then a left, then another right. But he's behind us the entire time.

"Thank God," Daphne says, blowing out a relieved sigh. "The guys are here." That's when I notice an SUV behind the car chasing us.

Sophie's phone chimes. "Benson wants us to pull over."

My eye widen at the thought of Carter getting so close. But before I can fully panic, Sophie turns back to me.

"Just so you know, this isn't going to be pretty. Not only is this guy fucking with one of us, he's got all three of us in this car. I hope he believes in God." Then she turns back around as Daphne pulls onto a side road to pull over. The three of us swing our heads around to see the car go speeding past with Finn's SUV right on his tail. Another car pulls up behind us, and I'm about to absolutely lose my mind from fear when Paul steps out of the passenger side and charges toward us. The car that he just got out of squeals as the tires grip the pavement and speeds away.

Paul opens my door, motions me to scoot over, and then jumps in next to me.

"Who's that?" Daphne asks, pointing at the back of the car Paul was in.

"Don't worry about it. My house. Now."

His deep commanding voice is scary, and we all know that Paul isn't messing around. Daphne quickly puts the car into drive.

"Give me your phone."

He stares at my shaking hand, then his eyes flick up to mine, and I swear Paul looks like he could explode from rage. Finally, he takes my phone and goes through all of the text messages that Carter sent me. His face only gets scarier as the glow from the screen in the dark car highlights his angled features. The phone goes dark, and he slides it into the inside of his suit jacket.

"I'm going to need that back," I whisper. "I'm going to have to call my parents."

"Not tonight you don't."

"You can't just take my…" I get cut off from a throat clearing in the front seat. I can see Sophie perfectly in the front and she has her head in my direction. When I catch her eye, she ever so slightly shakes her head, signaling to me that it would be bad to argue right now. She's probably right. I'm a freaking mess anyways, and Paul looks on edge to say the least.

Paul rushes all three of us into his building and doesn't look like he even takes a breath until we are all inside his empty place. Daphne and Sophie sit on the couch, but I can't sit down. How did this even happen? How could I be so stupid and give a stranger my phone number? The second we were secured inside, Paul went straight into another room. I hear him barking orders, but I can't make out what they are. Walking over to the large windows overlooking the water, I can't help but think that I've brought this chaos into all of their lives. The cold glass stings my arm as I lean into it, hypnotized by the dancing lights of the city on the water. I hear Paul come back into the room.

"Benson and Finn are on their way up."

A slight relief takes over knowing that at least they are okay. They must be really pissed off for me dragging their wives into this mess.

"Did they catch him?" Sophie asks.

That's the only time I turn my head in his direction. His eyes meet mine as he shakes his head, looking angrier than ever. Daphne and Sophie stand up and grab their purses.

I push off of the window and begin walking toward them.

"You aren't going anywhere," Paul says.

"This entire mess is all my fault. I mean, for crying out loud, we were in a high-speed chase tonight. You could have gotten hurt, your friends could have gotten hurt. All because of me. The safest thing I can do for all of you is to go to the police and stay away from you."

Paul closes the space between us, and he places his hand on my hip. He bends his neck and almost touches my nose with his. "You. Aren't. Going. Anywhere."

I'm about to argue until I feel his thumb begin to move up and down slowly on my hip bone. He only used to do that when something was serious. I already knew this was a serious situation, but I didn't know until this moment how serious it was for him, too.

"Okay."

"Okay," Paul repeats, then blows out a rush of air as Finn and Benson walk in the door.

I turn to see Daphne and Sophie with wide eyes and huge smiles. How can they be smiling after what just happened?

"I'm so sorry," I say openly to the room.

"Don't apologize. You're part of the circle now. We take care of each other no matter what," Daphne says as she wraps her arms around me.

Sophie comes in to give me a hug and whispers in my ear, "Paul doesn't look it, but he's fragile. Let him keep you safe. For both of your sakes."

I nod, but it brings on yet more questions about Paul and how he got to this place of misery. It also brings another side of guilt for adding to his barrel full of issues.

"I'll call you as soon as Paul gets you a new phone and, knowing Paul, it will probably be here before you even wake up in the morning."

Oh God. Wake up in the morning. *I'm spending the night here.*

"Is everybody okay?" Finn asks, checking over Daphne, then Sophie, then me.

Finn is a huge guy. I would never want that man coming after me. His arms are the size of my entire waist. The three of us nod. Benson walks over to me and places a hand on my shoulder.

"It's been a long ass time, Jolene. It's good to see you."

I haven't seen Benson since high school, but he doesn't look any different than he did back then. He and Paul were always together and we hung out a few times.

"You, too. I'm sorry for tonight."

"It is not your fault. We'll get this taken care of," he says.

—

With everyone gone, Paul and I are alone in his cold empty condo. The only thing warm about it is the view from the windows. It's my favorite spot and I have a hard time staying away from them.

"I don't think I should be going to the gala tomorrow night."

"Tell me one thing."

"What's that?" I ask.

"Do you want him back?"

"Luke?" My voice heightens. "No. Absolutely not."

"Then what's the point?"

"I promised Billie. My word means something to me. It just so happens that he is going to be there too, and I refuse to give him the gratification of introducing me to his new fiancée as I stand there alone."

"Then we're going," Paul says. He pours a dark red liquid into two wine glasses, then walks over to me. "Here. I think we could both use this."

I grab one of the glasses and tip it back, sipping the contents. I should have known that it was going to be sweet. Paul joins me in leaning one side against the glass. As we stand together, bodies facing one another, it starts to dawn on me how quickly all of the guys got to us.

"How did you get to us so fast?"

Paul immediately looks away from me and out the window. He takes a sip from his wine glass and continues to ignore my question.

"Paul. How did you get there so fast?"

His head angles to the floor and his eyes peer up. "We had a bit of warning that something wasn't right."

"How?"

The anger begins to build within me. I can barely stop the tears from forming in my eyes. I already know how. This was the demise of the two of us back then. I can't believe he's done this again.

"You had me followed. Didn't you?"

"Fancy, let me explain."

"No. God damn it," I yell and push myself away from the window.

"For once, I'm not going to apologize. It was a good thing Everest was there watching you. Otherwise, who knows what could have gone down tonight. Who could have gotten hurt. Or worse. You want to be pissed, fine. Be pissed. But I won't apologize for protecting the ones I love."

"Oh, thanks a lot. As if I didn't feel guilty enough for putting Daphne and Sophie in danger."

"I'm not talking just about them, Jo. I'm talking about you."

My body stills. Did he just say that he loves me?

"You should have told me. I feel like we are having the same fight only years later."

Paul sets his wine glass down on the only coffee table he owns. "This is different." He rubs his hands over his face, then sits on the couch. "Back then I was just a jealous kid. Now I'm a protective man. And I knew something wasn't right the second I saw the billions of text messages on your phone. So I have someone I trust keeping an eye on you."

"That must have been it," I say to myself.

"What are you talking about?"

"I felt it. I knew someone was watching me when Billie and I were at the boutique getting my dress for the gala."

Paul sits quietly for a second. His jaw moves slightly back and forth, the muscle in it pulsing. With a face full of rage, he says, "Everest didn't start watching out for you until after that."

My throat feels narrow as I fight to swallow the lump that has formed in it. "Oh God."

"Get comfy. You're staying with me until we find out who this is."

"What do you mean *find out*? I have his name and phone number. Can't you track him or something?" It's apparent by his expression that Paul is still not telling me everything. "Tell me."

"We haven't been able to track him. Everest is the best guy I know at tracking people down, and he can't find whoever this is. Benson and Finn couldn't catch him. My gut tells me that we aren't dealing with some dude off the street with a crush."

The reality of what Paul is saying only brings more fear. I've never been one to make the right decisions. Thank God my father flew out this afternoon.

"We need to call the police," I say.

"No. No cops. I'll find him way before they will anyways."

"Why don't you want the cops involved?"

"I think we both know my reputation with the police. Besides, Everest and I are better at this than they are. And even if they do find him, they won't do anything."

"Really? And what are you going to do?"

Paul sits quietly, and I watch the crimson liquid empty into his mouth. He smacks his lips together, making a sound. I get an uneasy feeling in the pit of my stomach.

"Paul. What are you going to do when you find him?"

"Make good on a promise."

He gets up from the couch before I can say anything and grabs my wine glass on his way into the kitchen.

"This is not happening."

My life was a disaster before creepy stalker guy even came into the picture. There's so much going on, it feels like there are a ton of bricks on my shoulders.

"Until we find him, you aren't to be alone."

"Well, that's just great. You do realize that I live alone, right?"

"Then stay with me."

"With you? All the time? Here?"

Paul gets that devilish grin on his face. "We could always stay at your house."

He knows damn well we can't stay at my house. If my father comes back or—God forbid—my mom shows up, I can't even imagine what they would do. A frustrated groan comes out of my mouth.

"This is just such a damn mess."

I pull my hair roughly out of the elastic and begin pulling each section out of the braid. My hair, now wavy, spills into my face as I place my head in my hands. I'm scared. I'm frustrated. I'm lost. Paul's hand slides through my wild hair, and his warm touch encloses on the back on my neck. The thumb movement is all that's needed for the tense muscles in my shoulders to relax.

"It's going to be okay, Jo. We'll just be connected at the hip for a little while."

"No, we won't. I'm hoping to have a new job soon. I'm pretty sure I didn't apply anywhere that has a bring-your-buddy-to-work policy."

"We'll get it figured out. But this weekend, it's you and me. And we are going to that gala because you promised your friend. You don't break promises."

With a slight pull from his hand, my body slowly lowers until my head is on his lap. The TV turns on, but I don't know what he's watching because the gentle stroking of my hair puts me into this magical spell where the horrible world melts away. I can't tell you how long we sat like that on Paul's couch. It was at least a few shows before Paul turned the TV off and the entire space was dark.

"You awake?" he whispered.

"Barely."

My eyes refuse to open, but I feel my head lift off of his lap and set on the cushion below. Five fingers touch my ankle as he removes both of my socks. I can't believe he remembers that I can't sleep with socks on. I moan quietly from how good it feels having them off of my feet. Paul's arm scoops up my knees as his other snakes under my back and he lifts me off the couch. Without much thought, my head rests against the front of his shoulder.

"I could've walked," I say, yawning.

"I know."

Paul's bedroom is just as stark as the rest of his home. There's a bed, a nightstand with a lamp, and a TV. He lays me down on his giant bed, amongst his black bedding. The cool soft fabric gives me a chill, and my shoulders twitch. Paul turns to the dresser and pulls out a white t-shirt.

"We'll hit up your house tomorrow, so you can get some clothes and your dress for tomorrow night," he says as he hands me the shirt to put on.

"Paul. Tomorrow I'm going home and I'm calling the police. I know you're intentions are good. But I don't want any part of your illegal plans."

His face sinks further with each of those words. But I can't go back there again. It was one of the things that drove us apart. He knows that I was raised to follow the rules, and the only time I ever broke them was when I was with him. He makes a gesture between the shirt and me, then turns his back. Quickly, I remove my blouse and pants, throw on the t-shirt, and toss my clothes to the side of the bed.

"You can turn around."

Paul comes to the bed and sits on the edge.

"This isn't the way to handle things, Paul."

The warmth in his eyes grows frost right in front of me. It shoots a pain straight to my chest.

"Give me until Monday. After that, you do what you want." He pulls the blanket up to my chin and tucks it on the sides. With his head inches from my face, he stills. He wants to say something, but he's hesitating. I can practically see the fight he's having with himself. It's probably the same fight I'm having with myself.

"We've both been down a long road," I say quietly.

"Don't go there. You have no idea what I've been through." He twists off the bed and turns to the dresser as he unbuttons his shirt.

"Then tell me."

Paul remains silent, and I watch as he walks from the dresser to the bathroom. He shuts the door and I can hear the water running. I know he isn't going to talk about it anymore. He could never bring himself to talk to me about his parents either. I sink deep into his bed and shut off the lamp. I wish I could figure out these feelings I have. On one side, Paul makes me absolutely mad. The other side is where my heart lies and, as usual, when Paul walks into the room, my heart jumps. He sets something on top of the dresser, then the sound of his footsteps leave the room. Faint sounds from the TV filter in through the open bedroom door. I have seen the pain in Paul's eyes, but I've never seen how he shuts people out until tonight. He shut me out.

—

"Come back."

My heart is beating so fast it feels like its knocking against the walls of my chest. Paul yelling from the living room catapults me out of the bed.

"No! Come back to me," he yells louder.

I peek around the corner into the living room to see Paul twisting and turning in his sleep. I flip on the light and run to the side of the couch. His body glistens from the sweat that is dripping down his forehead. My hand gently shakes his arm.

"Paul?" My voice comes out as soft and calming as I can make it. "Wake up, honey."

His body violently jolts awake, and his eyes grow wide as he sees me in front of him. He clears his throat and quickly gets up from the couch. Unsure of what to do, I stay on the floor as Paul paces across the living room. The black basketball shorts he has on are so low on his hips it looks like they could fall off at any moment. With each twist and turn of his body, his muscles contract and show themselves. He wipes his hand across his forehead to rid himself of the sweat. I do the only thing I can think of. I'm not sure he even sees me as I get up from the floor and head to the bathroom. Opening the cabinet, I find a hand towel and make it damp with cool water. Paul hesitates when I come close, but once I put the cool rag against the back of his neck, he stills. His head falls down, and he lets me cool him down. Slowly, I move to the front of his body and place the cool towel over his forehead before gently wiping down his face. His eyes are closed as he relaxes with my touch. They open slightly as the towel and my hand begin to lower across his chest and down to his stomach. Cautiously, I look to him. The worry must be obvious.

"Thank you. I'm fine," he says.

He takes the towel from my hand and walks into the kitchen. I'm still standing in the living room where he left me. Paul takes a glass from the cabinet and fills it with water from the front of the refrigerator.

"That must have been one hell of a nightmare," I say.

"I'm fine. You can go back to bed."

My body moves by itself, one step forward. "What was it about?"

"I said," Paul's teeth clench together and I can see the anger rise within him, "I'm fine!"

Paul has never raised his voice to me. The shock of it sends me straight back to the bedroom. My feelings about what just happened are so conflicted. I'm angry at Paul for yelling at me when I was just trying to help him, but at the same time, his tortured soul was showing, which breaks my heart. Once I'm in the bedroom, I shut the door. A loud crashing comes from the kitchen, and I know it's the glass he just had in his hand. As quietly as possible, and with my heart beating fast, I crack the door just enough to see into the kitchen. With both of his elbows on the island, he's leaned over with his hands covering his face. Slowly, he moves his head lower, and his fingers grip onto his hair as if he would love nothing more than to pull it all out. If I didn't know Paul, I would feel the need to get as far away from this ticking time bomb as possible. But I can't. The love that I had for him never left. I tried so hard to get over him, and I was doing an okay job until he showed back up on my front stoop. The trick to this is how to help Paul without him pushing me away.

His sudden movement brings me out of my thoughts and racing to get into the bed. I curl up into the sheets with my back to the door of the bedroom. The air changes as he walks into the room, and I grip onto the blankets tighter. He was so angry only a moment ago. His heat warms my back as the bed dips behind me. He's silent for a minute and I'm nervous to speak.

"I'm sorry."

Surprisingly, Paul's voice is back to controlled and deliberate.

"I forgive you," I say quietly.

Paul leans over and kisses my forehead before leaving the bedroom again. I doubt I'll sleep at all. There are so many questions that are looming overhead, and I want answers. Whatever is tormenting him is far stronger than the will he once had. After everything that happened tonight, I'm determined to find out what is haunting Paul. Even if that means he'll hate me in the end.

Chapter
Eleven

—

Paul

The fresh air does nothing to relieve the anxiety from the nightmare last night. I walk with my head down, analyzing the cracks in the sidewalk on the way to the coffee shop. The nightmares have always been horrible, but I've never awoken in such a panic before. It was like the world was closing in on me, and this time, I was the one that was moving further away instead of the faceless woman. Seeing Jolene when I opened my eyes sent me into overload. I was so angry that anyone had seen me like that. It's never the persona I wish to show the world. I learned a long time ago to never show people how to kill you. Weakness is death.

There's a lot of guilt also swimming around in my head. I yelled at her. She doesn't deserve that. It only solidifies that I'm not the man she needs me to be. But that doesn't mean that I'm not going to do everything in my power to make sure that she is safe. She's been just as much a victim of me as Heather was.

"Sir?" The barista at the coffee shop around the corner from my condo grabs my attention.

"Sorry," I say, before ordering two coffees. One with a splash of milk and one sugar, the other a caramel macchiato with an extra caramel.

As I walk back to the condo, I begin to obsess over this gala tonight. What if that creep is there? What if he tries to get to Jo? I want to call Everest for an update, but I don't have a spare hand, so my mind begins to run wild. I know Everest has already spoken with Gill. This asshole has no idea who he's messing with.

The condo is still quiet when I walk in, just like I had hoped it would be. I set the coffees on the island before slowly opening the bedroom door. The sight paralyzes me in place. I should have stayed out of this room. Her body is slightly sideways, facing me, and one leg is out of the covers and hanging off of the bed. Even though only the skin of her leg is exposed, she looks so beautiful with sunlight shining in the windows behind her. It's staggering how I feel about her here, in the place that I've kept everyone out of. The one place where I don't have to hide the pain I feel inside. Her eyelids flicker a bit before she opens her eyes slightly. The sweet smile that crosses her face when she sees me doesn't help the tightening in chest. I want nothing more than to go to her. To feel her against me. But today could be a dangerous day, and I need to think clearly and keep my wits.

"I got you a coffee."

"Thank God," she says, yawning.

Her body tilts to the side as she sits up, and her perfectly messy hair flows all around her face. She stretches her arms out, twisting her back, causing her breasts to press against the white shirt. I'm about to throw wits into the breeze and climb into this bed with her. Knowing I have to get out of this room, I pivot on my heel and head to the living room.

A few minutes pass before Jo comes into the living room and reaches for a coffee cup. I keep trying to message Everest, but he hasn't been responding.

"Oh my God," Jo chokes. "This must be yours."

Since I was distracted and on the phone, I never paid attention to which cup was which.

"Yep, this one's mine."

She cautiously takes a drink from the other cup and then smiles contently.

"How do you remember all of this stuff? The greasy cheeseburgers.

How I like my coffee. I can't remember what I had for lunch yesterday."

"I'd never forget anything about you, Jo." Only a second of silence passes before I realize what I said out loud. Her almost painful stare sends me scurrying to play this off. I shrug. "I pay attention to everything. Most things you want to know about someone, they never have to say."

Her eyes break from mine. She takes another sip.

"I have to meet Billie at the hair salon at eleven. Are you going to sit next to me the entire time?"

"No. I have a little business that I have to take care of this morning. But you'll be safe."

Her brows furrow and she looks suspiciously at me. "I don't want to be watched. I'm already creeped out enough."

I'm doing my best to not freak Jo out, but making sure she is safely monitored at the same time.

"Finn has agreed to keep close to you while I'm busy today. I figured you would approve of him. He's not going to be watching your every move inside the salon, but he's going to be very close by, and if you run into any kind of issues or trouble, then you will just call him and he'll be there in seconds. It's the only way that I can give you what you want and I'll know you are safe."

I'm surprised when she nods in agreement. That went over much easier than I expected it to. Jo was always a little feisty when it came to me, but she has always been quite the people pleaser.

"I'll need to go to my house first and get the things I'll need for tonight, like my dress."

I had almost forgotten about the dress and how she teased me with it. Well, at least there will be one thing to look forward to this evening.

—

I drive around Jo's block twice before feeling confident that no one is here watching the place. I made a point to look in every car parked along the streets and the few people that were walking down the sidewalks.

The small of Jo's back feels damn good under my hand, but I'm trying to pay more attention to our surroundings as Jo unlocks the front door and we head inside. She begins running through the house, grabbing things from different rooms, and placing it all by the front door.

"Do you need help?" I ask. I've taken a seat in one of the chairs in the living room.

"Nope," she says, running upstairs.

The tone of my phone ringing is muffled in my pocket.

"Hey," I say to Benson.

"Do you have everything you need this weekend?"

Damn am I thankful for these people who have my back. It brings a smile to my face that these men have stepped up to help me out.

"Finn is going to keep Jolene company while I'm working out some shit with Everest today. Then I'll be with her from then on. I might need some backup in the office come Monday if we haven't gotten him by then."

Fuck. Why did I just tell Benson I was working with Everest? Benson understands that there are certain people that I still communicate with. But that doesn't mean that he likes it. In fact, he hates it. If it were up to Benson I would never talk to any of the guys that were locked up with me. The phone is silent for a minute.

"You're in love with her."

"Stop," I say to Benson. Jo comes into the room and gives me a curious look. I cover the speaker of the phone with my hand.

"I'm going to take this outside. It's just business," I tell Jo.

Once I'm outside and out of earshot of Jo, I sit on the top step.

"Your wife has one hell of a big mouth."

"Sophie didn't say anything about you and Jolene. Did you tell her that you're in love with Jo?"

"Whatever I might be feeling doesn't matter right now. I refuse to have this conversation."

Benson gives an audible sigh. He knows what this feels like. It wasn't too long ago that Sophie was in danger, and Benson wasn't playing around with anyone when that was going on.

"You're right. Whoever this bastard is doesn't seem to mind that he scared the hell out of three women. I don't think he realizes what kind of men are attached to those women."

"Oh, I'm sure he doesn't. The men that are looking for him right now have no conscience."

"With Jolene's safety in jeopardy, I'm not going to lecture you on the company you keep," Benson says, "but you know how I feel."

Benson knows this isn't the time to challenge me about who I have looking for Carter right now.

"I hear you," I say.

"Sophie did say something about everyone coming out to the farm, or I should say mountain house. She's really excited about it. You and Jolene should…"

"No."

What felt like a refreshing breeze when I first stepped out of Jolene's house now feels like painful little pinpricks on my cheeks. Even the mention of the mountain house turns my blood cold.

"C'mon, Paul. You can't do this forever."

"Oh yeah?"

"Fine. You tell Sophie you aren't coming."

Benson knows Sophie is one of the few people who can talk me into doing things I really don't want to. But not this. There's no way in hell I'm going anywhere near that land again. Not after seeing that box of dreams that Heather left behind. Not after those words I read.

"I have to go. I'll see you Monday at the office."

"How about I just handle the damn office until you are certain Jolene is safe again. Do what you have to do. Just remember one thing."

"What?"

"It wasn't your fault."

"Why are we going back here? We've had it out about this years ago. I thought we came through the other side. I'm not about to go another round with you, Boss."

"Accept the facts and don't fuck this up with Jolene. Face it. She brought color back into your face. Means the blood is pumping again."

Benson hangs up before I can say anything more. Damn him for knowing me so well. I check the time and head back inside to help Jo finish gathering her things.

———

After dropping off Jolene at the hair salon with Billie and making sure that Finn was nearby, I drove to the coffee shop where I'm waiting for Everest, Gill, and Whack. Setting down the coffee cup after draining the entire thing, I see the three men walk in. Everest looks the most intimidating. He's built big and has a permanent sour expression on his face. Everest was named after his great-grandfather. Gill's story is a sad one. He was attacked as a young man by a couple of boys from his school. They had been bullying Gill for years and they caught up to him one night as he was walking home from work. After punching him repeatedly, they held his head under the water in the fountain. Gill held his breath and pretended to be unconscious. When they let go, Gill snapped up and put both of the boys in the hospital. A story was concocted, and since Gill was the loner in school and the boys were on the lacrosse team, not one person stood up to defend Gill. Nobody believed him. The parents of the boys who attacked Gill pressed charges and the judge decided to make an example out of him. Unfortunately for Gill, he was over eighteen at the time. Poor kid didn't have a chance. When he came into the pen and told everyone his story, one of the guys teased him about having gills and being able to breathe underwater. That's the day he became Gill instead of Mike. I'm pretty sure it's also the day that Gill lost his belief in humanity. Slowly he became the beast everyone said he was. The two of us have a lot in common, which is probably why we connected so quickly. We both were given no other choice than to be bad. Truth be told, I don't even know Whack's real name and I'm not sure anybody really does. He was a feared man in jail. I just tried to keep to myself, do my time, and get the fuck out of there. Normally, I would have avoided a dude like Whack. But his loyalty to Everest is stone solid, and since Everest and I are close, Whack and I are too.

All the men sit around a small table, elbows on the surface, and hovering over their cups of joe. As I look at each of them around the table, I can't help but think about how Jolene would flip if she knew what I was really doing. But after I saw that fear in her eyes and watched her hand tremble with terror, I'll do whatever I have to ensure her safety.

"Early this morning, Carter sent Jolene a text message. He apologized and said he was just being stupid. What he did was wrong and he asked her to forgive him."

Whack speaks up with his deep baritone voice. "What did she reply?"

"I've had her phone since last night, and I don't intend for her to know anything that we've talked about here." I look seriously around the table to make sure the men all understand what I'm saying. Not that they would ever talk directly to Jolene, but they need to know that I won't be talking in front of her about the situation. "Gill, did you get the new phone?"

"Of course," Gill says, handing me over a phone that looks identical to the one Jo has. I don't know where he gets these phones so quickly, but if I don't ask, then I don't know.

"So what's the plan for tonight?"

Everest nods to Whack. "He'll be in the back and I'll be sitting in the front. Anything happens, we'll be at your side in seconds."

"What about Gill? What's your plan?" Part of the reason Gill was teased so much in school was because he always had his head in his computer. If only those kids realized what Gill is capable of. He's practically a genius and can do things on that computer that I wouldn't even know where to start.

"I'm close to getting a lot of details that I need to nail down who is bothering Ms. Jolene. Once I'm confident in my findings, I'll give the info to the boys."

I know when Gill says "the boys" he's talking about more than just the three men sitting in front of me. My connections are with Everest, Whack, and Gill, but they have many more connections that I don't know about. Everest knows I only ask for help when I really need it. When it's important. He also knows that I don't want to know any of the other details. I trust him, and that's all I need.

As we walk out of the coffee shop, Gill and Whack give a nod, then scatter in different directions. I feel the weight of Everest's eyes on me. Turning to him, the cold wind hits my face and bites my skin.

"You sure about this?" Everest asks.

"Of course I am. You know I don't fuck around, Everest. Whoever this is deserves whatever he's about to get."

"I'm not talking about him."

"Nobody messes with the people I…"

"Jesus Christ. Have I taught you nothing, boy?"

I clear my throat and lean against the brick wall of the coffee shop. "You remember that girl I told you about whose dad blackmailed me away from her?"

Everest nods.

"Jolene is the girl."

I told Everest a long time ago how much I loved the girl that I had to leave. I just never told him her name. He doesn't say anything but gives a knowing nod. "I'll be in touch." And with that, I know Everest realizes how important this is to me.

I pull up to the side of the road, and Finn comes walking toward me. He opens the passenger door and gets in.

"Anything?" I ask.

"Not a thing. It's been real quiet. I checked in on her through the window a few times, and she was laughing with her hairdresser. You really think this idiot would come back after the scare we gave him?"

"My gut says yes."

Finn and I exchange a look, but something catches our eye. A stunning woman walking out of the beauty shop, her long curls bouncing with every step her petite legs take.

"Looks like you're going to have a great time tonight," Finn says, laughing.

"Hey, Finn," Jolene says. I watch as she places a friendly hand on his arm as he helps her into the car.

"You two behave tonight," he jokes. Then his face loses his friendly smile and his fierce protective nature shows. "If you need me, call."

"Will do," I say as he closes the door and I pull away.

"Are you all set for tonight?" Jolene's sweet sultry voice fills my car.

"Of course. Are you?"

She smiles, but her eyes are missing the touch of shine they usually have.

"What is it?" I ask.

"I'm a little nervous."

"It's understandable. He's your ex. There's bound to be some awkward feelings involved."

"I'm not nervous about him," she squeals and looks at me as if I have lost my mind.

"Then what the hell are you nervous about?"

"The dress I bought with Billie. I'm not sure I can wear it."

"Why not?"

Jo shifts in her seat. "Never mind. I'll figure it out."

—

"We're going to be late," I shout into the bathroom where Jolene has been for the last hour.

After we left the beauty shop, we came back to my place. Someone might assume she's staying here for a month with all of the shit she brought with her.

"I can't wear this," she shouts back. "Hand me the other dress bag that is laying across your bed please."

"Let me see it."

The bathroom door cracks open barely enough for her red lips to peek out at me. "Just give me the other bag."

"I recall someone teasing me with a picture of this dress. If you don't want to wear it, don't. But I think it's only fair that I get to see it before you change."

The smirk that was on my face fades as the door swings open and Jolene stands in front of me looking more stunning than I have ever seen her before. The air expels from my lungs and I struggle for it to return.

"Why the hell won't you wear that dress? You look beautiful."

A dusty rose fills her fair cheeks as she does the look that drives me crazy. Her eyes look to the floor as she pushes the hair that falls into her face behind her ear. I want to stop myself, but my legs carry me close to her. My hands reach out and touch her soft skin. The black dress with red lace flowers flows over her curves. The deep cut in the neckline makes my tongue circle inside of my mouth. The heat between us increases as she inches closer and presses against me. Her eyes blaze and look deeply into mine as her breath gently blows across my jawline. Standing here, dressed for a fancy gala and seeing her looking to me for strength, I vividly remember why I can't have her. She's too perfect.

I take a casual step back and focus on the problem at hand. We both try to play off what we felt.

"There's nothing wrong with that dress, Fancy."

Her eyes falter as she slowly begins to twist her body around. *Fuck me.* I've never seen Jo in a dress like that. The slow spin reveals the problem isn't the dress. It's the lack of one. I try to ignore every instinct I have to rip that dress off of her and never leave this condo.

"Paul!" she shrieks, snapping me out of the daze this woman has had me in for the last several years. "Get it together. What am I going to do? A lot of people my parents know are going to be at this gala. Can you imagine my father's face if I wore this dress? I don't know what I was thinking letting Billie talk me into this."

"Want my opinion?"

She rolls those beautiful eyes. "I already know it."

"Wear what you want and stop being so worried about how others perceive you. No matter what you do, someone won't approve. If wearing a dress that shows a little skin in the back is too much for you, then don't. We really need to go, though, so you might want to decide quickly. I'll be in the living room."

As the minutes tick away, I try to get the image of Jolene in that dress out of my head. I wanted to tell her that those people are asinine and, if anyone said anything other than how gorgeous she looks, I would rip them to shreds.

"Let's go before I change my mind," she says, walking quickly out of the bathroom. She snatches up her handbag, then flings the door open and races out.

As Jolene stands in front of the elevator in my foyer, all I can see is the backside of her. Although she still has on the same dress, there's now a black shawl draped over her shoulders covering the once-exposed skin. The younger Paul would have convinced her to skip this event. But that isn't what she needs. She needs someone who is going to live up to all those standards that have been drilled into her head. Someone…safe.

Chapter
Twelve

—

Jolene

The limo pulls up to the fancy downtown hotel. An older couple gets out of the car in front of us. Their faces look familiar, but I don't know their names. I knew what I was getting myself into when I had agreed for the second year to attend this gala for Billie. I knew that I would be rubbing shoulders with many people that my parents know.

"You ready for this?"

"As I'll ever be."

The limo door opens, and Paul steps out, then reaches for my hand to help me out. It doesn't matter how many of these events I've been to, I still get anxious for every single one of them. Always have to put on such a show. Fake perfection. Kiss all their asses and make them think that my family is retaining their elite status within the community. If it wasn't for my parents, I wouldn't care. And if it wasn't for Billie, I wouldn't even be here.

As we walk through the lobby, I'm taken aback by Paul. He walks with such confidence and strength. He nods and smiles politely at other guests we pass. I'm so mesmerized by him that I don't notice I've dropped the fabric from the front of my dress and the tip of my pointed shoe catches on it. Paul's bicep tightens as he swings his other arm around and places a hand on my stomach, catching my fall. With wide eyes, I stare at him. If I had fallen in front of all these people, I would have been mortified. Before I can say thank you, he winks at me. Scared to fall again, I watch the toes of my pointed high heels kick out from under my long dress as we make our way to the designated ballroom.

We stop in front of the open double doors that lead directly into the ballroom full of people that are mingling around the decked out room. Purple and white lights illuminate the space and shine off the crystal chandeliers. I turn to Paul for reassurance, but see him straightening the collar of his white button-down shirt. It's the first time I notice a twinge of something in his eye.

"Are you nervous?"

"Don't be ridiculous."

His hand presses against the small of my back as he ushers me into the space. The tables are adorned with bright white table clothes and dinner settings made of classic white dishes and dark purple napkins. Crystals sparkle brightly through the tall glass vases filled with water and a floating candle. The only piece of tableware I care about is the wine glass. I'm going to need that full and hopefully quickly.

"Jolene," a voice from behind grabs my attention. "It's so wonderful to see you again. Thank you for coming. It means so much to Billie and me."

"I wouldn't have missed it. This is Paul. He's the CEO of Knoxx Developments. Paul this is Samuel Bennet, Billie's husband. He's a doctor at the hospital and co-chairs the Heart Gala."

He reaches out, shaking Samuel's hand, and they begin a quiet conversation about the current real estate market in Boston. I see Billie excuse herself from a conversation and walk toward me with a huge grin across her face.

"You look amazing," she says, wrapping her arms around me. Although we are still standing with the guys, we've turned slightly away from them to have our own conversation. "Although, I can't help but notice that you decided to cover up this evening." Her left eyebrow raises as she playfully smiles.

"I almost didn't wear the dress at all." I left out the part about how I would have let a bear gnaw off my right foot so that I wouldn't have had to come at all tonight. From the mean stare aimed over my shoulder, I could have said it because she wouldn't have heard it.

I turn and scan the room in the direction of Billie's glare. It doesn't take long to spot him. Luke stands at the side of the bar, talking with a group of men. A strange feeling takes over, and it's nothing how I thought I would feel seeing him again. Before I can turn back around to speak to Billie, I hear my name being called from my right.

"Jolene! How wonderful to see you."

"Hello, Helen. It's nice to see you again as well."

Helen Merriweather is one of my mother's best friends.

"How are you dear?"

"Oh, I'm doing all right. How about yourself?"

Ugh. This forced small talk is enough to make me want to run out the doors.

"Well. To be honest, I'm a bit concerned, dear. I saw you walk in with a date this evening."

Unable to hide the confusion in my voice, it pitches high. "Yes. I have a date this evening."

"It wouldn't be that Paul fellow, would it, dear? Your mother is so upset after the phone call from your father."

Now I know that Helen is my mother's best friend. But that gives her absolutely no right to butt into my personal life. I'm about to forget any manners that I may have been brought up with when a tall man with a friendly smile walks up to Helen's side.

"I don't think you've ever met my son, Kyle. He's an orthopedic surgeon. Kyle, this is Jolene Barrington."

It's not out of the ordinary for me to have never met Kyle. In my mother's circle of friends, a lunch date without children was their usual time together. As I grew a little older, she would bring me along from time to time, but none of the women ever brought their sons. I'm not sure that I like the way that Helen is looking between Kyle and I. The way she grinned as he appeared at her side would suggest she has more in mind than just a friendly introduction.

"It's a pleasure to meet you, Jolene."

Kyle grabs my hand gently and brings it up to his lips as he kisses the back of my hand. I almost forgot how completely exhausting and fake these events are. It makes me sick how all these people try to act so prim and proper, but behind closed doors, they are the same assholes everyone else is.

"Nice to meet you too." I hope that my nonchalant response and lack of eye contact are enough to show my disinterest. No sooner did the words leave my mouth and I can almost feel the eyes from a beast growing behind me.

"Your mom and I think the two of you have a lot in common. You know, Kyle is off for the weekend. Maybe a coffee date is in order? What do you say, dear?"

Of course my mother would be trying to put her hands into my life from all the way across the country. I was trying desperately to just make it through the evening for Billie. But now, I regret every single minute of being here. Turning, I see Paul's eyes on me just as I had thought they were. I jerk my head slightly, signaling for him to come to me. But he doesn't. He just takes another drink from his champagne flute and resumes speaking to Sam. *Why would he ignore me like that?* It was clear from the look on his face that he didn't like the interaction between Kyle and I.

"Glad to hear you've kept in touch with my mother since they moved."

"Oh yes, dear. I just spoke with her this morning. She suggested the introduction."

The annoyance cascading through me is becoming harder to conceal. Billie walks by just in time for me to grab her.

"Billie, I completely forgot to grab you that drink."

"Drink?" Billie looks puzzled but only for a minute before she sees my pleading eyes.

"Oh yes. I was waiting for you up by the bar. I'm glad I found you." Then she turns to Mrs. Merriweather and smiles.

"It was nice to meet you, Kyle. And it was so nice to see you again, Helen."

I tug on Billie's arm, and we walk away from the wannabe matchmaker.

"What's the deal?" Billie asks as I lead her quickly toward the bar.

"She was trying to set me up with her son. With my own mother's blessing by the way."

"Oh geez." Billie laughs.

I get a glass of champagne and watch as the bubbles leave the bottom on their way to the top.

"I tried to get Paul to come to me, and he wouldn't."

"He wouldn't?"

"There was a look in his eye. Like he didn't want to come into the conversation."

Billie purses her lips, and I follow her eyes as they look over my shoulder. Paul is standing behind me.

"Billie, can you give us a minute?" Paul asks.

"Of course. I'll just go see how the auctions are doing. I'll catch up with you in a little while."

I nod and turn to Paul. He looks uncomfortable.

"You want to give that guy a chance?"

The words had to soak into my head for a minute before I fully comprehended what he just asked me. With the crowd and the music, there is no way I would have thought that Paul could have heard that conversation.

"No." Even though there was nothing wrong with Kyle, my face contorts in disgust.

"He's a doctor. Your parents approve. He fits right into this lifestyle."

Now I get it. Just as I'm about to grab his hand and tell him that none of that matters to me anymore, his phone rings.

"What is it?" he answers.

My body goes numb from the adrenaline that I didn't notice was rising within me. I was about to tell Paul that I can't think of anyone other than him. Turning to the bar, I slam back the remainder of my champagne and order another one. I'm going to need something to help me get through this night. When I turn back to Paul, I see his eyes wandering the room while the phone is still pressed firmly to his ear. His eyes stop at someone by the door.

"Noted. On my way." He hangs up and places a hand on my hip. "Stay by the bar. I've got to take care of something real quick, and then I'll be right back."

"Is everything okay?" I ask.

"Just business. But I want to be able to find you, so do me a favor and just stay put. I'll be back. Five minutes tops."

Feeling a bit defeated, I nod my head and watch as he mentions something to Sam just before he walks out the double doors. There's still a bit of time before the dinner begins and I already wish this night was over. I have every intention of getting the hell out of here as soon as I can.

"You look gorgeous." The clear, baritone voice gets louder as he walks to my side at the bar.

"Hello, Luke."

It was inevitable that our paths would cross at some point in the evening. I pause to gather the courage to face him. Meeting my ex-husband's new fiancée isn't high on the list of things I want to do. But I'm an adult and I've been raised with manners. So I take a calming breath and turn, only to find him standing in front of me alone.

"Where's your fiancée?"

What in the ever loving fuck is wrong with me? That is not something I wanted to ask out loud. Embarrassing warmth covers my face, and I can only imagine how red my skin has actually turned. I can assume it's pretty noticeable from the quick smirk that shot across his face.

"Um," he starts, scratching his temple with his index finger and squinting his eyes. "She's um...sick. Yep. She's not feeling...that's a lie." Luke's eyes quickly glance at the people who are within earshot of us. "We've decided to take a break," he whispers.

"I'm so sorry to hear that."

I'm really not sorry at all.

"I've been wanting to talk to you."

I take a sip of my champagne, and my eyes go to the emcee as he picks up the mic on stage.

"Oh yeah," I say, distracted. "About what?"

A warmth covers my right hip as he places his hand dangerously low.

"About us."

Stunned, my vision goes from the emcee to his hand on my body. "Don't touch me," I warn, and I brush his hand off.

"You never wore anything like this before." His index finger touches my collar bone and begins tracing down the deep V-cut hem. "I've missed…"

His touch doesn't get very far before agony covers his face.

"You ever place one fingertip on her skin again and I will make you pray for death."

Paul's low threat isn't noticed by anyone, as they are all enthralled by the emcee. Paul is so close to Luke's back that I didn't see that he had Luke's other arm twisted behind him until he let him go. Luke straightens his suit jacket and presses his lips together in disapproval and maybe even a little embarrassment. Lucky for me, I couldn't care less what he thinks. Paul wraps his arm around my waist and pulls me away from Luke. I barely hear the emcee as I am staring at Paul in disbelief.

"Couldn't be helped," Paul says, his hand resting on the small of my back and continuing to lead me to the other side of the room by Billie. "Stay here with Billie. I'll be right back."

"Paul, don't." I grab ahold of his arm in fear that he's going to confront Luke again.

"Relax, Fancy. I'm just going to get a drink. Don't worry, he's not at the bar anymore."

Looking back to the bar, I scan the people standing around. He's right. Luke isn't anywhere in sight.

"What the hell is going on?" Billie asks.

"Luke got a little handsy. Paul showed up and nearly broke Luke's arm."

"Oh good. I knew I liked him," she says with a grin.

Oddly enough, I think I liked it too. It felt amazing to have someone stick up for me. To feel protected. I wanted to show Luke that I was a different person. I think I did that. But as my mind races through my feelings, the heat within me grows as I realize how I'm truly feeling. My eyes dodge through the people in the crowd until they find their target. Paul has a drink in his hand, but he looks to be in a conversation with someone. I can't see who because of a man blocking my view. His expression is one of concern and maybe even a hint of disappointment. That's when the crowd moves and Helen Merriweather appears next to Paul. The glass in his hand rises, and he empties the contents into his mouth. He wipes the corner of his lips with his index finger as his head nods reluctantly. Our eyes meet and my stomach drops. Nobody is going to tell me who I can and cannot be with. Not anymore.

"Billie," I say turning to her. "I love you. But…"

"Go."

"I'm so sorry."

She grins wickedly and pulls me into a deep embrace. "Just get the hell out of here. Take that man home."

She must have noticed my eyes turning from playing nice to dangerous. The kind of dangerous that only Paul can bring out in me. A chill creeps up my spine as I drop my shawl and lock eyes with Paul. One of his eyebrows rise and I can tell he isn't hearing anything Helen is saying anymore. My breath quickens as part of his bottom lip gets sucked into his mouth. My legs don't stop until our bodies touch and my lips press intently onto his. Helen's voice is only a murmur in the background. Paul's hold on me tightens as his tongue swirls against mine. I'm reluctant to break our touch, but I can't stand being here with these people anymore.

"Take me home," I whisper against his lips. "Let's go now."

That devilish grin that I always swooned over appears on his face. After taking a few steps toward the exit, I look back over my shoulder to see Paul still standing next to Helen. Her expression is one of disbelief as she shakes her head in condemnation. Paul's eyes have grown dark and hooded. They travel the length of my body and, once they reunite with mine, he moves to me. His hand presses against the bare skin of my lower back and begins to lead me out of the room.

Just before we clear the exit doors, I see Luke watching me from the corner. Paul gently pushes on my back to speed up my pace. Once in the hallway, Paul pulls out his phone and presses a few buttons. The night breeze sends a shiver down my arms while we wait for the driver to pick us up.

"I can't believe you did that."

My heart stops as the words came out of his mouth harshly.

"I'm sorry?" It comes out as a question because I'm not sure which part of the evening he's upset about. Or why he would be upset about any of it. "I didn't do anything. Luke just came up and…"

"I'm not talking about that dick. He knows now not to touch what's mine." Paul nonchalantly looks down the road.

"What's yours?" I ask.

"You walked through every person in that crowd with eyes only for me in that damn dress. Looking dangerous as fuck. I could barely control myself. You're mine."

Laughter bursts out of my chest.

"You laugh now. Because the only things coming out of your mouth for the rest of the night are moans and my name."

Chapter
Thirteen

—

Paul

Jo's warm cheek presses against my chest. I wonder if she notices how rapidly my heart is beating beneath the skin. Yep. It's there. I can feel it. Silk strands of her long hair flow through my fingers as I stroke from her forehead to the ends. This moment could be the most serene I've felt in years. It's also much different than when we walked out of the elevator tonight after coming home from the gala. Jolene's dress was half off before we even made it out of the foyer and into the living room.

The guts she had to make her point could have brought me to my knees alone. But then she walked at me with those determined eyes, and there was no stopping her. I never wanted to change Jo. I fell in love with her exactly the way she was. Did I encourage a little adventure? Sure. But that was never to change who she was or what she valued. I became her escape. One that she so desperately needed. And still does.

Jo moves, situating herself up on an elbow. Her leg is still happily laying across part of my body. I haven't been able to get the smirk off my face since we climbed into the back of the limo. But as soon as I see Jo's concerned eyes sparkle with the tiniest amount of moonlight coming in through the blinds, it disappears.

"You okay?" I ask.

"What did she say to you?"

I cup part of her cheek in my hand and my thumb strokes her sweet skin. "Doesn't matter."

We both know, it matters to Jolene. It matters because tomorrow isn't going to be pleasant for her. She's going to have to deal with the backlash of her family. She's a grown ass woman and she should be able to do whatever she wants without having to worry about what her mommy and daddy have to say about it. But that just isn't the reality of Jolene Barrington's life. Nobody wants to purposefully disappoint their parents even if they're sixty years old. I remember the look on my mother's face the day they came to arrest me. The horrified look on her face is etched in my memory forever. I never want to see that look on her face again. The second I could afford it, I bought her a place in California. She was born there and always wanted to go back. More so after everything that happened with me. Even though our relationship has never been the same, and we don't talk much anymore, I wanted so desperately to make her happy. So I get it. But Jo needs to do what is going to make her happy at this point in her life and stop worrying so much about approvals and the reputation of her parents that no longer even live in this city.

"It does matter."

"I know you're worried about what your parents are going to say, but it's going to be okay."

I stroke her skin with my thumb.

"My parents? I'm worried about you."

"Why would you be worried about me?"

Jolene puts her hand over mine and presses it firmly against her cheek.

"What happened to you after us?"

Her whispered voice echoes in my empty room. All of these people who have become family to me over the years have begged me to talk. I never talk. Maybe it's because the thought of Jo making her own scenarios in her head make me more nervous than telling her the truth, but my mouth opens.

"Benson had a sister. Her name was Heather."

The pain that came out with my voice when I said her name was uncontrollable.

"I remember he had a sister," she says.

"We snuck around for a while. We were nervous about what Benson might have to say. It's one of the rules. Don't date your best friend's sister."

"So, Benson got upset?" she asks. So innocent. If that was the only thing that happened, I might not be as fucked up as I am.

"He was."

"What happened?"

"There was a lot of fighting. Between Benson and I. Heather and I. I even fought with myself. Then things got really bad. Because of all the disagreements, Heather and I broke up. At first, I just thought that she was upset about the breakup. But it became clear that there was much more going on. She had somehow gotten involved with this guy and he was bad news. Benson thought I was the bad one, but he had no idea that by telling his sister that she wasn't allowed to see me anymore that he would be leading her into the arms of a druggie. She got addicted pretty quickly."

"I'm sorry. That must have been really tough to watch."

I stare up at the white ceiling. "When their dad died, she spiraled even more out of control. She begged for me to come back to her. But I couldn't. I told her there was no *us* until there was no more drugs. She didn't choose me. And that was my fault."

"That was not your fault," she says strongly. "You can't take responsibility for that."

"If I would have gone to her. Told her I loved her and talked her into the help she needed, she wouldn't be in the ground."

"Paul…"

"They found her lying on the ground in a fucking alley with that scum. Both dead. Overdose."

She places a hand over her mouth. "Oh Paul. You can't—"

"I've failed everyone I've ever loved." Tilting my head back to the side, I take in her eyes as she watches me spill my guts out. "Including you."

Her head falls and she places it onto my chest. She leans over and places a soft kiss on my lips before she lays her head back onto my chest. Silence again reigns in the room and, on the inside, I break. She didn't argue. I did fail her. I failed Heather. I failed Benson. I failed myself. I've known all of this for a long time now. The only difference is, she's still here. She didn't leave. She didn't look disgusted. She touched her beautiful lips to mine, then laid her head across my heart. She's one hundred times a better person than I. The question is, how do I make sure I don't fail her again without telling her what her father has done? What I have done.

—

Light shines through the cracks of the wood blinds in my bedroom. My eyes adjust slowly to the brightness as I wake up. I slept. I slept the entire night without a nightmare and I'm relieved. It scared Jo when she witnessed the nightmare, and I never want her to be scared. Not when she's with me. The black covers are dipped low, exposing the entire area of her back as she lays on her stomach. Her long dark hair is sprawled across the pillow in my direction. A musky vanilla scent fills the air from her hair conditioner that she used last night. It smells so damn good. I could watch her laying peacefully in my bed all day. But someone has other ideas.

Jolene's cellphone begins chiming on the nightstand next to her. A small, quiet groan comes out of her mouth as she stretches her arms and legs out. The chime goes off again. She grabs the phone from the nightstand, looks at it, then puts it back. Her beautiful eyes come to mine. Damn she looks so good in the morning. Leaning into her, I place a kiss on her lips. Another chime from her phone echoes in the room.

"Ugh," she groans.

She grabs it again off the nightstand, sits up with the covers tucked under her armpits, and begins slamming the screen with her fingers.

"It's my mother."

"You don't say?" I tease.

She smiles and finishes her text. "I'm going to have to call her in a few minutes. What do you want to do today?" she asks.

"I thought I would take you out to dinner."

Then she does it. She does that look that has always driven me wild. The one where she dips her chin low to her chest, closes her eyes, and blushes. As if she is so enamored with the idea of going on a date with me.

"Like on a date?"

I nod. I nod even though guilt sliced through me. I wasn't prepared for it even though I've felt it living deep in my gut since my hands brushed against her sweet skin in the pub. The excitement in her eyes hasn't darkened, so I must have done a good job at hiding it.

"You call your mother. I'm going to make us some coffee."

I kiss her warm, soft lips before leaving the room.

Every few minutes, Jolene's voice gets loud enough that I can hear it through the closed bedroom door. She's been on the phone talking to her mother for the last thirty minutes. I haven't been able to make out any of the words, but I can only imagine what they might be. The door opens and Jolene sits on the couch next to me.

"Coffee?" I ask.

She nods. "I don't really have anything to wear on a date tonight. I only have jeans and casual shirts."

"I'm wearing jeans and a t-shirt."

"Wait. What? You are going to wear jeans?"

"I'm not sure where the confusion lies here."

"Mmm-hmmm." Her playful grin makes me smile.

—

Pale pink tight jeans grace the seats of my car. The dark hair that is usually cascading down her shoulders is tousled up into a poufy ponytail. Unlike last night, her makeup is light, allowing for her natural features to shine through. I'm angry. Angry at myself for making this damn dinner date and not keeping her at home all to myself today. The happiness that was on her face when she walked out of the bedroom to see me casually dressed was contagious. Though I still don't understand what the big deal is. My slightly distressed dark denim jeans pair perfectly with a white button-up shirt and a navy sport coat.

Light rain sprinkles on the windshield. I would have dropped her off at the door before I parked the car, but there's no way in hell I'm letting her out of my sight. Not until I find out who this asshole is that tried following her. I don't feel so bad about it once she begins to giggle as we jog, hand in hand through the parking lot.

Sitting across from Jolene and keeping my hands to myself seems like it will once again test my control. Nothing in the room could deter my eyes from watching her lips part and the pale white wine disappear through them. I can't help but to think about how good they probably taste right now. How cool those lips would feel against mine. I'm only torturing myself.

Halfway through Jolene's roasted chicken and my grilled steak, something catches my eye from across the room. Sitting back in the booth, I watch him for a minute to be certain that I'm seeing what I think I am. Feeling confident, I grab my phone and find the name I'm looking for.

"Don't freak out," I tell Jolene as I listen for an answer on the other end of the phone.

Her face contorts in confusion. She begins looking around her, then back at me.

"What do ya need?" Everest answers.

"You get a description yet?"

"Yep. Was going to call you in a few hours. About five-ten, brown hair, looks built but not like your buddy Finn. Smaller. Drives a black hatchback. That's it for now."

That was all I needed. Standing from the table, my eyes stay locked in on the guy sitting at the table by the bar.

"I need you to stay right here. Don't get up. Don't walk anywhere. No matter what happens, don't leave this booth."

Before she can protest, I walk away from her in the direction of the man matching the description that Everest just gave me. The blood heats in my veins as the adrenaline creeps into my bloodstream. I would love to smash that asshole to pieces who put the girls in danger. His brow furrows as I block his line of vision forcing him to look at me.

"What the fuck?" he asks.

"Who are you?"

I slam my hands onto the table about to question him when Jolene shouts my name.

"Paul! What are you doing?"

Her arm intertwines with mine as she begins dragging me away from the man's table. The entire restaurant has frozen. Everyone is standing in one place and looking at me as if I'm nuts.

"Jolene, this could be the guy," I whisper to her. "He was fucking staring at you, and I didn't like the look on his face."

"I don't know what the hell your problem is, buddy, but get the fuck out of the way," the man says from the table now behind me.

Jolene points in the direction of our table, and it's only then that I see the TV playing a sporting event in the reflection of the mirrors just above where Jolene was sitting.

Once we get back to the booth, Jolene's disappointed face pains me.

"You have to stop this. I think you've gone too far."

"Someone was stalking you. Then chased you down in a car. You don't see a problem with that?"

"I think Carter probably saw me by coincidence that night. Maybe he got a thrill from chasing us and thought it was funny. Smart? No. Malicious? I don't think so."

"Trust me on this. I have a bad feeling about…"

"I remember trusting you quite well, Paul."

Her eyes are full of fury and I feel like someone just knocked the air out of me. I know she has a point. But before I can explain why this time is so different, the waiter returns to the table. And he isn't alone. A woman wearing a tag with the word MANAGER under her name stands at the edge of our table.

"I believe that there was some sort of miscommunication, but unfortunately, I'm going to have to ask you to leave."

She looks incredibly uncomfortable, and I don't want to make a bigger scene for Jolene than I have already.

"It's okay. I understand."

The giggles that filled the air as we were walking in are now gone. We both walk slowly through the mist to the car. I can't let this go on.

"Fancy, I…"

She stops walking, turns to me, and grabs my hand.

"Look. I know that you feel like you are protecting me. I know that you genuinely feel like there is something more here. But don't do this. Don't ruin what we've rebuilt."

I nod and kiss her head to calm her. But she's right. There is something more going on here than Jolene cares to admit. I am protecting her. And nothing in the world is going to stop me from doing that.

Chapter
Fourteen

—

Jolene

The air in the elevator on the way up to Paul's condo is thick with tension. We didn't speak another word after Paul kissed me in the parking lot of the restaurant. I know he wanted me to stop talking. Truth is, I love the fact that Paul feels so adamant about protecting me. He can't go back down that path again. I won't let him.

Echoes of my shoe clicks ring out as we walk into the condo. Every time I hear something echo in this place, it reminds me that Paul has been punishing himself. For years. It breaks my heart.

His hands come from behind and wrap comfortably around me as I gaze out over the harbor. Soft lips touch the skin of my nape and a shiver slides down my spine. Goosebumps raise as he gently removes my long cardigan. Kisses continue from my neck to shoulder as the warmth from his hands increase the warmth already gathering below.

"I'm sorry," he whispers. The quick burst of air against my ear intensifies the desire. The thin bra under my sleeveless undershirt can't hide my hardened nipples. His mouth opens, briefly sucking on the skin at the base of my neck. A twinge hits my core as his hand grazes over my protruding nipples. With the twist of his index and thumb, I hiss. The bulge from his erection presses deeper into the curve of my back just above my ass.

Everything stops, but only for a second. His arms reappear on my body, but this time under my legs and behind my back. He carries me the few feet to the couch and lays me across. Before he can move very far away, I reach for his erection through his jeans. I free him of his pants, but he doesn't give me the opportunity to do anything else. My shirt is lifted over my head as I fumble with the button and zipper on my pants. The rubber band is removed from my hair and it tickles my back as it falls into its normal messy curls. Paul traces his index finger lightly down the center of my body beginning at my forehead, down my nose, continuing down my sternum and my belly button.

He grips my waistband firmly and begins shimmying my pants down my legs. I hear him pick up his pants, the packet rip, and the pants falling back to the floor. The constant throb that has developed below is almost unbearable until he touches me. His fingers work and glide inside. My breath quickens as he works in and out of me. That lip of his is getting sucked into his mouth as his hungry eyes take me in.

"Come here," I pant, pulling his face to mine. I lose the sensation of his touch, but it's renewed as his erection begins rubbing against me. His tip pushes against my opening, and I can't take it anymore. My hips push upward sending his erection further into my body, and he releases a deep groan from his throat.

"Oh, Jo."

We've had sex a few times now since being reunited. But up until now, it hasn't been like this. This is love. And I can feel it more in every tender touch of my body. He is worshipping me. Supporting me. Loving me. And I…

"I love you." *Oh God.* I said it out loud. That fear only takes hold of me for a second because the rush of something more powerful was about to overcome me. Paul picks up pace and locks eyes with me. I can see the struggle he's having to keep it together. To wait for me. He isn't going to have to wait long because a million bursts of light shoot through me. A high like no other surges through my body. There's no stopping the moans that come with every thrust. Paul groans quietly as he releases and joins me in orgasm.

The rush has passed, but neither of us have steadied our breath yet. He places his hand on my cheek and deeply kisses me. Gently, he pulls his body off of mine. Leaning down, he places one more kiss on my lips.

"I love you, Jolene. Always have."

Then he walks out of the room and into the bathroom. Now not only do I feel like a limp spaghetti noodle from being so exhausted from our fit of passion, my heart is in a big melty puddle on the floor. He loves me.

—

I woke up this morning to two text messages, a voicemail, and a letter on the pillow that Paul slept on last night.

> *At work. The lobby knows that no one is allowed through security up to this condo other than you. I connected your laptop to my Wi-Fi so that you could use it whenever you wanted to. Stay here. If you need something, call me. I'll be home later this afternoon.*
> *-P.*

The first text message is from my mother asking if I've located my mind yet. Actually, I located it the minute I stopped worrying about what makes them happy and started thinking about what makes me happy. The second one was from Sophie asking us to come to the mountain house this weekend. I hope I can talk Paul into going out there. It sounds like it would be so much fun and get me away from the city.

After listening to the voicemail from the doctor's office I applied at, I called them back and was offered the position. Maybe things are starting to work out just as they should. I sit up in Paul's big, cozy bed and my eyes travel to his empty walls. Not one picture. Not even a piece of artwork. Maybe I can help with that. I grab my laptop that Paul set on the nightstand next to me and begin searching. My intention isn't to change him. Sure, he has his quirks. Everyone does. But Paul deserves to come home to place that's warm and comforting. And I don't think he's ever going to do that for himself.

Around lunchtime, I get a text from Paul.

> **PAUL:** *How is your day going?*
> **JOLENE:** *Amazing! I got the job I wanted. Only a few more days you can keep me locked up in this tower.*
> **PAUL:** *You aren't a prisoner. If you want to go your house, you can. I'm just going too. Where is this job at?*
> **JOLENE:** *It's downtown. Dr. Ray.*
> **PAUL:** *Tonight we celebrate. See you later.*

"See? This is what I love about Paul," I say to Billie.

"That's so awesome. I'm so happy for you. Quite a different response that nitwit would have given you."

I already know that Billie is talking about Luke. Luke didn't care about anything unless it was a benefit directly to him. He never wanted me to work. Instead, he wanted me to showboat around town just like my mother did. Meet friends for a stuffy, uptight lunch. Brag about our useless husbands by making up shit that never really happened. Fake a smile every time you turn around. No fucking thank you.

"You've got that right. Listen. I want to order a few things to surprise Paul with for his condo. Would you mind if I had everything sent to your house so that he won't see it beforehand?"

"Do I get to snoop in the boxes when they arrive? You know, for quality control?"

I laugh, "Actually that would be great. I'm hoping to get everything hung and in place in one afternoon before he comes home from work."

"Well, let me know if you need any help."

"I will, thanks."

"Jolene?"

"Yeah?"

"I'm so fucking proud of you."

She hangs up the phone and my own sense of pride wells up inside of me. I'm damn proud of myself too. I'm finally standing up for what I want. What I deserve.

———

Paul and I sit on the floor on opposite sides of the coffee table. The pizza box sitting between us is half empty. When Paul came home from work, I was sitting on the couch watching TV. He walked in with a pizza and a six pack of beer. Some girls wouldn't think this would be a romantic gesture, but he remembers. This is my favorite kind of evening. Leaning back on his hand with his legs stretched out in front of him, he takes a drink.

"So. Tell me about this job. It's with Dr. Ray downtown?"

"Yep."

"Perfect," he says, but quietly. I think he meant to say it just to himself.

"Why is that perfect?"

His guilty and determined eyes flash from his beer up to me. "It's close to one of my projects. I won't be far if you need something."

With all of the construction going on downtown that I passed on my way to the interview, I know that he's probably telling me the truth. But something says he's got more up his sleeve than what he's saying.

"I'll be working Monday through Friday, which I'm really excited about. Working at the hospital, you work whenever they need you to work."

"Eight-hour shifts?"

I nod, the excitement probably obvious on my face. I'm so damn excited.

"I hope this job is everything I think it's going to be. Then again, anything has to be better than the hospital."

"Is that why you quit? Because you didn't like the hours?" Casually, he brushes the crumbs on the table into a neat little pile.

"No. It just wasn't for me."

"Why not? What's going to be so different other than the hours?"

This is the last thing I want to talk about tonight. Silence comes over the room as I try to think what to say. But I've taken too long. His eyes jolt up from the crumbs on the table and squint at me.

"Those dimples on your forehead. Tell me."

Damn.

"Death is different."

Instead of that being the end of the conversation, he just continues to stare at me. I've never told anyone out loud why I couldn't go back. Billie was there, so she knew already. I take a drink of my beer, place the bottle on the table, and stare at my hands in my lap while I briefly relive the day that changed me.

"I clocked in for my normal shift. Myles was happy to see me because I was relieving him for the day. I didn't know him outside of work, but we had a great working relationship. A few hours into my shift, a gunshot victim came staggering in. I happened to be walking by and he collapsed into my arms. It took me a few seconds to realize it was Myles. He squeezed my hand and begged for his life. I can still hear his voice in my head saying he didn't want to die. By the time he came into the ER, it was too late. He died within seconds on the floor holding onto me. I just couldn't go back after that."

It's difficult to hold back the tears, but I'm desperately trying. I hate crying in front of people. Unable to take my eyes off of my twiddling fingers, I listen for Paul to respond. I hear nothing but suddenly feel a hand under my arm pit. With one arm, Paul lifts me from the floor and wraps me up in a tight embrace. I can't say how often I've felt like I just needed a hug. There was just no one there to give me one. The comfort overwhelms me, and a few tears slip out. But I have time to wipe them away because Paul doesn't let go right away. He holds on and gives me time to inhale his soothing scent.

"I'm sorry, Fancy." He releases only enough that we face each other. "I didn't know. I wouldn't have brought it up if I did. We're supposed to be celebrating."

"I'm okay." I actually feel better now that I've gotten that out. I'm not sure why telling the story out loud helped, but it seemed like it did. I give him a small smile.

"Dr. Ray's office is going to be good for you. I think you'll really like it there."

Confusion sets in. "How do you know that?"

He rolls his eyes and takes an audible breath. "Always too smart for your own good."

"Oh great," I say, teasing.

"Dr. Ray is a friend of Benson's family. He was close friends with Benson's dad. Because of that, I know him very well myself."

"You didn't have anything to do with me getting that job did you?" I say as I sniffle.

"Absolutely not. I didn't even know you had interviewed there. But at least now I'll be able to make sure you're safe even while you're at work."

I can't help but let out a frustrated breath. He's back to this again.

"Don't worry. It's going to be fine. Why don't we just relax for the rest of the night? Movie?"

Before I can answer, he places a soft, sweet kiss on my lips. As if I could say no to anything after that. He points to the couch for me to sit and proceeds to clean up the pizza box and our empty beer bottles. I flip through the channels until I land on a movie that's just beginning. I'm not even really interested in the movie, but when Paul sits down on the couch and pulls me into him, there's nowhere else I would rather be.

I'm shook awake by Paul's moving body. It takes me a second to realize that he's having a nightmare again. His body writhes and, even though his eyes are closed, the pain in his face is apparent.

"Come back," he says, his voice full of distress.

"Paul," I say gently. I'm scared to wake him up again because of the reaction he had before, but I can't stand here and watch this either. My hand cups his cheek and the muscles in his face, relax. His eyes blink rapidly trying to open.

"You're sweating. I'll get you a cool rag." Running into the kitchen, I grab a rag from the drawer and run it under the water. He sits up and leans over his legs, putting his head in his hands. I don't think he did it on purpose, but it was the perfect position to place the rag on the back of his neck.

"Thanks," he says.

I sit down next to him, not sure what to do. I want to know what these dreams are about, but I'm nervous that he'll just close up like he always has. I've only got one bargaining chip and I'm going to use it.

"What is it about?" I ask quietly.

"Don't." He never even raised his head. I can still see part of his face, though as he is resting his forehead on his thumbs.

"I told you mine. You asked, I told you. Your turn."

He turns his head and glares at me, but I don't budge. My shoulders are strong and my face is as straight as it can be. I'm not messing around. I want to know what the hell is haunting him in his dreams. His head returns to the same position it was before on his thumbs. Just when I think he isn't going to tell me, Paul's voice fills the air.

"It's the same every time. There's a woman in a white flowing dress. The skin on her long arms is porcelain white and so is her hair. The wind is strong, so it blows it all around her. The light is so bright behind her that it looks like she's glowing. Her hand is stretched in my direction and it looks so close. But when I reach out to grab it, it's just out of reach. No matter how hard I run, I can't get to her. She turns her head and there's nothing but a black hole where her face should be. Then she floats away so fast, I can't catch her. Usually I wake up before she's completely gone."

My insides hurt as he tells me every detail. I don't know how to respond to his tortured soul. I know who this nightmare is about and so does he. Words just don't seem appropriate right now, because nothing I say is going to fix this. So instead of even trying, I just grab his hand.

"C'mon. Let's go to bed."

I continue to pull on his arm until he sluggishly gets up from the couch and follows me into the bedroom. Once in there, I pull off his shirt. The gorgeous art that covers his chest makes so much more sense now. The clock with the skull below it. My fingers brush over the doves before I climb into the bed still pulling him behind me. I try to wrap my arms around him, but he stops me and instead pulls me into him. He kisses my forehead and pulls the covers over both of us.

"I love you," I whisper.

"I love you, Fancy."

———

"I just don't know if I'm going to be able to talk him into going. He said no already once before and it was a quick no."

Sophie sighs heavily into the phone. After his nightmare last night and finding out what it was about, I'm not sure I want to push the issue either.

"I can't say that I blame him," Sophie says. "But I really wish he could get passed it. The mountain house is such a special place for Benson. When Finn and Daphne come, we always sit around talking about how it would be nice to have us all together."

"I'll ask him again. I can't promise anything, but I'll try."

"You're a gem, Jolene. I'll talk to you later. Good luck," Sophie says.

"I'll let you know. Bye."

Setting my phone on the counter, I return to the lunch I made myself in Paul's kitchen. He didn't have anything in the fridge but the kind of beer I don't like. So I ran to the store this morning. I got really nervous when I felt like I was being watched again, but then I remembered that Paul is most certainly having me followed around. A quick text just to be sure confirmed my suspicion, and I kept on shopping. I'm not sure at what point I became okay with this arrangement. Perhaps it's because I've seen how traumatized he is and he honestly thinks someone is out to get me. At some point this charade is going to have to end. I'm not going to deal with this for much longer. I can't pick my nose without someone knowing about it.

Even though I've ordered a few things for Paul's surprise, I still feel like I'm missing something. Maybe something a bit more personal. Then it hits me. Excited, I grab my laptop and begin searching through all the pictures that Billie put online from the gala. I squeal as the picture she took of Paul and I comes up. It turned out great. I'll have this printed out and put it in a beautiful, but manly, frame. I know the perfect place for it in the bedroom on his dresser. That way he'll see it every morning when he wakes up. Once Paul is convinced that there isn't anyone after me and I go back home, he'll be able to look at it and remember that someone loves him. I hate to admit the feeling in my stomach when I thought about going back home was like a sickness. The past few days have been so good with Paul. Spending so much time with him has made us be honest and open with each other. More than ever before. Now my mind is racing and I'm making up scenarios in my head. Paul didn't start showing a lot of emotions to me until he had me staying here. So what happens when I go back home? Will things go back to the way they were? Will Paul go back to shutting everyone out? Then I remember Sophie's plea to get Paul out to the mountain house. I can at least try to use what leverage I have now to help him. I pick up my phone and text Paul. He's not going to like this.

JOLENE: *Sophie invited me to the mountain house this weekend. I'm going. I leave Friday evening and I'll be back on Sunday. Wanted to give you a heads up.*

Barely a second passes before those three little bouncing circles come up on the screen. I'm a bit nervous to see what he has to say.

PAUL: *Over my dead fucking body.*

Chapter
Fifteen

—

Paul

Pacing. I'm actually pacing in my office. The anger coursing through me makes my skin itch. Sophie would do anything to get me back out to that house. Thing is, it's not the house. It's what comes after. The last time I went to Vermont was for Benson and Sophie's wedding. I know Benson thought he was doing the right thing by giving me that box of Heather's. He didn't know what was in it, just that it had my name on it. It was filled with loose papers. Some were diary entries. Mostly about how much she loved me. Things she wanted to do. Dreams she had that would never come true. Then, there was the final entry. The one that placed the final shovel of dirt on top of my heart. Her perfect, beautiful curly handwriting explaining how I broke her heart and the only thing that helped ease the pain was the drugs. That was when the nightmares began. The mountain house is her house. It's where her spirit is. She is everywhere there. I'm trying to get rid of the damn things, not make them worse.

The chair squeaks as I sit in it behind my desk and take a few calming breaths. Once I feel like I've regained a bit of composure, I pick up the phone and call Sophie.

"Well, hello there," she answers.

"Not okay, Soph. What in the actual hell are you trying to do? Not only do you know how I feel about the mountain house, Jolene has some creeper out there and I need to make sure she's safe. And you've invited her to go gallivanting across the countryside."

When Everest called me during the gala to let me know that Whack had tracked down the vehicle and it was parked only a few blocks away, my determination to find this asshole has only increased. Thankfully, Sam is a good man and kept an eye on Jolene while I went outside to have a quick update from Everest. There's no way in hell I'm not having eyes on her. Not now.

"Listen," she scolds. "Whether you planned on it or not, Jolene is our friend. Daphne and Finn are coming out too, and she can ride with them. So if you want to keep your crabby ass at home all by yourself, then you do you. But Jolene will be just as safe out here with Finn and Benson. Daphne and I think Jolene could use a bit of a weekend away, and since she's starting her new job on Monday, it will be a good time to celebrate and enjoy each other. I don't know why you can't get out of your own damn way, Paul. But I wish someone would just punch you in the face to knock some damn sense into that head of yours."

I thought I was mad. Sophie raised her voice and she never does that. I feel like I just got reprimanded by my mother and now I should go sit in the corner. Not many know that I hate it when people I love are angry with me. And I don't like how upset she sounds.

"Soph, I can't. I want to spend time with all of you. You don't think I'd like to have a normal fucking life? I look at my two best friends who have everything I've ever wanted and, believe it or not, I'm starting to feel like I might be able to have it too. But no matter how hard I try, I'm reminded every day of the time that I've lost because I wasn't strong enough to stand up to her father and..."

"You were a kid, Paul!" Sophie argues.

"And I wasn't strong enough to stand by Heather until she could get herself clean."

"From what I know, that wasn't your fault either. That was a complicated situation and someone else's addiction isn't something you can control. If anyone knows that, I do. My mother chose her drugs over me. Left me alone in a hospital room to fend for myself. She never came back. At some point we have to stop taking responsibility for other people's choices."

"Everything is so fucking complicated."

Silence continues from the other end of the phone. I know she's there. Sophie is the mama bear of the group. Always looking out for everyone. Pushing us to want more and to do better. Even if that means tough love.

"She's so good for you, Paul." Sophie's voice is back to the soft, loving tone. "But if you can't give her all of you, the parts you pick and choose to give her won't be enough. You need to decide to give her everything or give her nothing. And if you string her along just to break her heart, she'll hate you more than ever before. You have to figure out if you can live with that."

"I...I don't know how. I don't know how to make the guilt go away."

A sad sigh comes through on the phone. "Face it. That's all I've got. That's my only advice. Face it. Confront it. Because it's obvious that ignoring it for so many years hasn't gotten you anywhere. So try something else."

"But that house. That land. That..."

"Oh, hang on," Sophie says, cutting me off. I can hear a rustling of the phone being moved around and another little voice.

"Uncle Pauwie?"

Damn her! Sophie knows that Katie could pretty much ask me for anything and I would do it. Luckily, my niece is still young and hasn't asked for a car yet.

"Hey, princess. What are you doing?"

"Pwaying with my dowwies. Will you come see my new woom? It's got pick walls!" Katie's little innocent voice could bring me to my knees.

"Pink walls? I bet it's real pretty."

"Yup. And it matches my new dwess too."

"Will you come? Uncle Finny is comin'. I wanna show you my woom. Pwease? Pwease Uncle Pauwie?"

My hand smacks hard against my forehead. All this pain and grief has kept me away for years and nothing was going to talk me into going back to that house. Except a toddler with a tight grip wrapped right around my finger.

"Okay, princess. I'll come see your room."

A shocking, inhuman-like scream comes through the speaker, nearly making my eardrum rupture. "He's coming! He's coming, Mommy! Uncle Pauwie is coming to see my woom."

I hear the phone hit the floor and Katie's voice soften as she gets farther from the speaker. I wait for a minute, and Sophie picks up the phone.

"So. We'll see you Friday night."

Her voice pisses me off. So damn chipper, and as if we didn't have that heart-to-heart conversation. She knew exactly what putting Katie on the phone would do and that it would work.

"You feel pretty damn proud of yourself right now, don't you?"

"It is an amazing feeling," she says. "See you Friday."

Maybe Sophie is right. I've tried everything in my power to ignore all of this for years. It hasn't worked and maybe it has gotten worse. I love Jolene and I want to make it work with her. I want to be with her no matter what. It's just this rogue feeling that I can't rid myself of and some days it spreads over me like a cancer. I don't want to live like this forever. Not anymore. Not since Jolene came back into my life and gave me a second chance. I don't want to ruin that. I won't.

I was a bit harsh when I texted Jolene last. The conversation that needs to happen can't happen while I'm at work. But I can't just leave it the way I did. With my phone still in my hand from talking to Sophie, I click on Jolene's name and start typing.

PAUL: *Sorry. I'll talk to you about it when I get home. Okay?*

I hit send and watch my phone to see if she's going to respond. That's when it hits me how concerned I am that she's angry. Going home and seeing her waiting for me in my living room was like coming home to the life I had pictured fifteen years ago. I don't want to lose it.

JOLENE: *I forgive you. But the next time you try to order me around like that, I'll give you blue balls for a week.*
PAUL: *That sounds like it could be interesting. Although, I highly doubt your ability to keep your hands off me.*
JOLENE: *You're ridiculous, and I could totally last a week. What time do you think you'll be here? I'm making dinner tonight.*
PAUL: *Six. Need me to bring anything home?*
JOLENE: *Nope. See you then.*

I wonder what she's making. I wonder what she's wearing. I wonder how she would torture me for that week. *Shit.* If I don't stop wondering, I'm going to have to leave work early. With my phone going off and Tina knocking on my door, reluctantly, I get pulled back into the busy day.

Instead of going back to the office like I usually would after a meeting that ended at five, the only place this car is headed is to my condo. I feel almost giddy to go home. A new feeling for me. Traffic in this town is one of the reasons Benson always hated driving here. He'll drive just about anywhere else in the freaking world but not in Boston. God forbid it rain or there be a wreck. It could add an hour or more added to the commute depending on where you're coming from. Thankfully, today my meeting was close to the condo because the traffic today was terrible. I pull my car into the underground parking that Benson insisted on for this building. Underground parking costs an astronomical amount of money, but now that I live here, I'm sure glad he pushed for it. I speed into my spot and waste no time getting into the building.

The elevator opens and the smell of home-cooked food fills the air before I even open the front door. I stand for a minute just outside and think about what it would be like to open this door to a wife and a kid or two running around inside. Good. I think it would feel damn good. And this is the closest I've ever been to even remotely accepting that it's a possibility for me. My hand anxiously turns the handle and opens the door slowly. I wasn't prepared for what was in front of my eyes.

Jolene's hair is up in a messy pile on top of her head. Her ass is barely covered by the black t-shirt she must have found in my closet. It only makes her bare, olive-toned legs look even longer. Music is playing from the speakers on the TV, but I can still hear the dishes clank in the sink as she grabs a plate out of the water. She swirls the rag around it before rinsing it and putting it in the drying rack. Unable to take my eyes off of her, my body reacts to the stupor my brain is in. The file I was carrying falls out of my hand, and the papers that were in it spill out all over the tile floor. It catches her attention. She spins around. Her fresh face shows the few freckles on her nose that are usually concealed with makeup.

"Oh my God!" she shouts. Her hands fly up to her hair and then to her face. "You're early. I wanted to be changed and put together before you got here. I'm a fucking mess."

I must look like a statue of an idiot. I swear I can barely move. Even though her beauty is unmatched by anyone else I've ever seen, she feels the need to still be better. I can see the panic in her eyes. It must be exhausting to constantly feel the need to be perfect. And on top of that, have such a skewed perception of what perfect actually is. She quickly steps over a few of the papers and tries to rush past me toward the bedroom.

"It won't take me long. I'll go put myself together."

My arm shoots out just in time to grab her around the waist and haul her to me. Against me.

"Absolutely not."

I grip her tightly around the small of her back, pressing my body further into hers. My nose grazes hers. It's difficult to stop myself from making love to her right where stand. I don't want to ruin the dinner she's made for me.

"But I'm a mess. I wanted this to be a nice evening."

There's no doubt she feels the heat coming from my body. I can tell just by the way she's licking her bottom lip and driving me absolutely crazy.

"This," I say, moving my eyes down between the two of us, "is perfect to me."

As the last word leaves my mouth, she closes any distance we had and her lips meet mine. My hand sinks into the back of her hair as I pull her into me, as if we could be closer than we are. The taste of her sweet lips and the damn smell of vanilla from her skin make me crave her. With just a little lift from my arm around her back, she hops up and wraps her legs around me. A small moan comes from her throat as she presses against my pants. I begin walking us to the bedroom when the timer goes off on the oven.

"Fuck it," she says, breathless.

Oh God. What I wouldn't do to ignore that goddamned timer right now. But she cooked me dinner and there's also that little thing about burning down my condo. Besides, she's the perfect dessert. She grunts playfully as I turn around and walk us back to the kitchen. I place her on the counter and kiss her lips.

"We've got all night. Let's not ruin your hard work."

Pulling open the drawer next to the oven, I grab the pot holders and pull out a casserole dish from the oven and set it on top of the stove. I'm not sure what's under the cheese that sits on top, but I don't really care. Jolene could make me a mud pie and I would probably eat it.

"Looks good," I say.

"It's just baked ziti. Not a big deal."

She places her hands on the counter and begins to scoot toward the edge. Before she can jump off, I move to her and help her down. I place a kiss on her lips and then move out of her way. She opens the fridge and begins grabbing more ingredients out.

"Do you need any help?"

"Nope. Go change."

"Change? What's wrong with this?" I look all over the front of my black button-up collared shirt and black dress pants.

"Oh, trust me," she says. "There's nothing wrong with that. But if I look like this, I can't sit in front of you looking like that." Her hand motions in the air over my body.

Smiling, I nod and turn to the bedroom. Time to make the playing field fair.

Chapter
Sixteen

—

Jolene

The coffee table was set. Each side has a plate of ziti, a fresh salad with vegetables, and bread. The only thing missing is forks. Running into the kitchen, I grab two and turn to head back to the living room but freeze as soon as Paul walks into view. I don't know how I missed the indentions on his hips before. He walks closer to me, casually in his boxer briefs.

"You're in your underwear." His finger flicks the hem of my t-shirt up. "I'm in mine. Now we're even."

Paul mentioned the other night walking out of the gala that he could barely control himself. He's right. Now we're even because I'm having a real hard time controlling myself right now. He grabs the forks from my still frozen hand and turns his back to me as he walks toward the living room. With each step, different muscles in his body tense and make their appearance. It's the biggest tease I've ever seen and he doesn't even do it on purpose.

"Looks so damn good, Fancy."

I try to shake off how captivated I am by him. But the second I walk into the living room and see him sitting so carelessly on the floor angled in my direction, I lose any appetite I had for dinner. His hooded eyes watch my steps as I walk directly to him. He bites his bottom lip and I'm done for. Once I'm within his reach, his hand starts at my calf but quickly moves up my leg as I push forcefully against his shoulder, causing him to lean back. The pressure of his erection through his boxer shorts presses against me as I straddle him on the floor. He places both of his hands on my ass as he stands from the floor still holding me up. The woodsy scent of his cologne only makes me want him more. My tongue runs up the side of his neck toward his ear.

"A week, huh?" he teases. He tilts his head to the side giving me more access to his neck as he walks us into the bedroom. Playfully, he tosses me down onto the bed and gazes over me with the sexiest smirk I've ever seen. "You didn't last an hour."

A giggle escapes me knowing he's referring to the blue balls I told him I would give him for a week. "Neither did you."

"With you, I couldn't last a minute."

—

Last night was incredible. Eventually, we reheated dinner and ate on the couch wrapped only in blankets. Just before I fell asleep in Paul's arms he told me he loved me. But when I woke up this morning, something just seems off. There was no note on Paul's pillow like the other mornings. I sent him two text messages and I didn't get a response for over two hours. I don't expect for him to be at my beck and call, but it's very odd from the way it's been recently. My phone chirps and I nearly fall out of the chair, reaching for it.

> **PAUL:** *Busy day. Be home late.*
> **JOLENE:** *Okay. I love you.*
> **PAUL:** *Love you.*

I wish his reply eased the weird atmosphere that I woke up to today. It doesn't. Something just seems really off and I can't put my finger on what it is.

I try to keep myself busy by planning out where everything is going to fit in Paul's condo. With the measurements all written down in a safe place where he won't find them and ruin the surprise, I watch a few home DIY shows on TV. I wouldn't be able to tell anyone what they were about, though. My thoughts have been with Paul all day and what's really going on. My phone rings and I spring for it, hoping that it's Paul and everything that I've been feeling today will have been all in my mind. When Daphne's name comes up on the screen, I can't help but be just a little disappointed.

"Hey, Daphne," I answer.

"I heard that you guys are coming to the mountains on Friday. I can't believe the impact you've had on…Paul?"

It was obvious that something caught her attention other than our conversation.

"You still there?" I ask her.

"Damn. I really thought he wouldn't come in today."

"What are you talking about?"

"I'm at work. Paul just walked in. Shit, girl. I really thought this would be it for him. I better go."

The lump in my throat is nearly impossible to swallow.

"Okay, talk to you later," I spurt out and hang up before she can hear the hurt in my voice.

It's Wednesday. I didn't realize that it's Wednesday when I woke up. It feels like we've been together and working through our issues for years because we've known each other for so damn long. I can't believe how fast we've been drawn back into each other's lives and how deeply that happened. But it's hard not to feel like it's not enough. He still struggled all day. He still went to the pub instead of coming here to me. He's still so broken.

The hurt I feel is for both of us and the tears can't be held back anymore. Sitting on the couch of Paul's empty condo, I sob. It only lasts a few minutes before anger takes over. I refuse to let him do this to us again. I refuse to stand by and watch him deteriorate every week at that damn pub. I know who he is and what he wants and if I have to drag him out of there, that's what I'm damned well going to do.

I throw on my sweater, grab my purse, and run out the door. Once in the lobby, I grab my phone and begin calling a taxi. The urgency to get to Paul makes my palms sweat so I head outside and begin walking quickly down the sidewalk.

"Jolene," an unfamiliar deep voice comes from behind me. "Jolene, stop."

Turning I see a huge man rushing at me. Fear takes over and so do my legs. I begin to run as fast as I can. But I'm no match for his long legs and he catches me right away.

"Get off of me! Help!" I yell and kick.

"I'm Everest. I'm Paul's friend, Everest. Are you in trouble?"

Looking at him with wide eyes and my heart beating so fast, I swear it kept running away from my body when he stopped me. But Paul told me about Everest. It's not a name someone could just make up to get to me so I believe him.

"No. I'm not in trouble," I tell him, placing my hand over my heart. "You scared the shit out of me." I take a few deep breaths trying to calm myself.

He squints at me then gives me a side eye. "Been cryin'?"

Why do men squint their eyes when they try to analyze something? What pisses me off about it is usually they're right.

"I'm fine. But I need to get to O'Reilly's pub and fast. My taxi should be here," I say, looking down the busy road.

"Oh no. You ain't gettin' in no taxi. Or out of my sight. I'll take you."

Part of me would love to stand on this sidewalk and argue with Everest about driving me anywhere. But the other part of me just wants to get to Paul as quickly as I can before he's had a few drinks in him. I nod and follow Everest to his car. He has a bag full of something in his front seat, so he directs me to the backseat and opens the door for me.

As the town passes by out the window, I bite my nails from the overwhelming anxiety of what I'm going to say to Paul.

"Did something happen? Paul okay?"

I'm so caught up in my own head that I don't notice Everest watching me in the rearview mirror. His brows are drawn in close together. He's calm, but suddenly the atmosphere kicks up a notch when he mentions

Paul.

"He's fine. I'm just about to go kick his ass."

Everest flashes his bright white smile at me. "All right. I'm going to park and we'll walk in together. Don't take off. I want eyes on you all the time until I see Paul's got you. Hear me?"

"You are all out of your minds. I can't believe how far you've all taken this. I swear, Carter is harmless."

There's no response from Everest. I huff loudly, and I roll my eyes as he opens my door once we've parked. We walk around the building and through the front door. Everest towers over me, and I know he's scanning the room for Paul just like I am. Daphne spots me just inside the door and waves for me with a huge smile on her face. I rush up to the bar, Everest on my heels.

"Where's Paul?" I ask her.

A puzzled look comes over her face. "He left right when I got off the phone with you. I was shocked he wasn't staying. He said he was going home to you."

The phone in Everest's pocket starts going off. He pulls it out and answers it.

"Yeah," he answers. His eyebrows raise as if he's amused. "She's with me. We're on our way." He hangs up and briefly tips his head toward the door indicating we should go.

"Oh shit," I say. "I'll talk to you later, Daphne."

"See you Friday." She smiles and heads with a beer to a table.

Everest drives me back to the condo and walks me to the elevator.

"Thank you, Everest."

"Jolene," is all he responds with a nod.

The ride to the condo in the elevator seems to take forever. I was so worried about Paul and that feeling changed to happiness as soon as I found out he didn't stay at the pub. The elevator doors open, and I walk out, but run right into Paul's strong body. He wraps me into a tight embrace, and I feel his rapid heartbeat and ragged breath. As our bodies separate, I can see the panic in his face before he grabs my hand and pulls me into the condo.

"Are you okay?" I ask. He takes my bag out of my hand and tosses it to the floor. I kick off my shoes, and he again takes my hand and brings me into the bedroom. He sits on the edge of the bed looking up at me.

"You were gone."

"I went to get you. I was fine."

He blinks rapidly, and I can tell he's fighting something within him. "You were *gone*."

I walk to the side of the bed, remove my clothes, and climb under the covers. Paul follows my lead and does the same. He wastes no time grabbing me and pulling me as close to his body as he can. The tight hold he has on me doesn't loosen until much later when I hear his breath even out. It's alarming to me that Paul was so scared when he came home and I wasn't here. Between his reaction and Everest being so determined to keep me next to him, I'm beginning to feel that there's something they aren't telling me.

—

I'm so excited to leave for Sophie and Benson's mountain house tonight, I've barely been able to sit still all day. Yesterday, after Paul came home from work, I confronted him about this whole thing with Carter. He told me not to worry and that he would tell me anything I want to know this weekend. We watched TV, and then Paul took me to bed and showed me how much he loves me.

Daphne and Sophie called me this morning to make sure that we were still coming. I called Billie to ask her about the things that have arrived already at her house. If the other night gives me any clue, I think I'm going to have to let Everest in on the surprise. He's got hawk eyes on me and I'm sure he'd tell Paul something was up if he didn't know what it was.

My phone chimes from the kitchen counter, and I race to it.

> **PAUL:** *Five minutes out. You ready to go?*
> **JOLENE:** *I was ready when my eyes opened this morning.*

I've already gathered the things I'm taking with and placed them by the door. As I wait for Paul to walk in that door, it crosses my mind that I've been here for a week already. Other than the Wednesday hiccup, every day has felt so natural and exciting. What's going to happen when he feels like I'm safe again? Will I go back to my parents' house?

The door opens and pulls me out of the negative thoughts swirling around in my head. Smiling, he comes to me, wraps me up, and kisses my lips.

"I've just got to grab a few things. Then we're off." That sheer happiness that was on his face when he first saw me falters slightly. I know him well enough to see he's trying to hide his nerves. Even though it's exciting for me to spend the weekend with the girls and see the beauty that Sophie has tried to describe, I know this isn't going to be an easy trip for Paul.

Guys are so much easier. They have to pack like three things for an entire weekend away. There's just so much more that a girl needs, like makeup, a curling iron, and a few options for clothes each day. I'm pretty sure Paul barely packed enough clothes to last him the weekend in his one little bag.

It was already dark by the time we got close to the house. But the sun was out long enough for me to know the trip to Vermont was a gorgeous one. We stopped at a quaint little restaurant about halfway through the drive. We turn onto a tree-lined road vaguely lit up by the moon. Lights appear on the horizon, and as we get closer, they illuminate a beautiful and large white home. Paul shuts the engine off and a sigh escapes him.

"Let's go," he says.

We walk up to the wraparound porch, and I picture how lovely it would be to sit on the rocking chairs and drink lemonade in the summer. It's dark outside and I can already see why Sophie loves it so much. Paul opens the door and motions me to walk in. As soon as he closes the door and turns to walk into the house, something miniature in size flies past me.

"Uncle Pauwie! You came to see my woom."

"I told you I would, princess."

He snatches a little body up from the floor and wraps her up in his big arms. I watch as her light brown curls bounce with each step Paul takes. He smiles at me as they walk past, and I can't help but to stare. Her little arm is wrapped around the back of his neck and she giggles as he whispers something in her ear. Still standing at the front door, I'm pretty sure that my ovaries just exploded.

"I'm so glad you guys made it." Sophie seems to appear out of nowhere and startles me. "Sorry, I didn't mean to sneak up on you like that." Her eyes follow mine to Paul with Katie. "Trust me. I know exactly what you're thinking. Wait until you see him with my baby boy. He's going to make the best daddy someday. C'mon in," she says, linking her arm in mine.

The interior of the house is stunning. As I walk further in, a large stone fireplace takes center stage. On either side of it are wide windows that stretch all the way up two stories. To the right of the living room is the kitchen where Daphne is opening a bottle of wine.

"Hey. Look who decided to show up," Daphne teases. She begins pouring wine into three glasses that are sitting on the biggest island I've ever seen.

Still holding the little girl, Paul opens a high cabinet in the corner of the kitchen. Even he has to get on his tiptoes as he pulls something out from the top shelf. "Yes," he hisses playfully. He opens the bag, pulls out a cookie, and hands it to her.

"She's so adorable," I say.

"I can't believe how rude I am. This is my daughter, Katie." She turns to Katie, who now has chocolate cookie all over her mouth. "Katie, this is Jolene. Can you say hi?"

Daphne pushes a wine glass to Sophie and me.

"Hi, Jowene." Her attention turns to Paul. "Let's go to my woom, Uncle Pauwie."

"Where are the men?" Paul asks.

In unison, Daphne and Sophie respond, "Man cave."

"Pink room, then man cave. Perfect," he says.

With Katie situated back on his hip, he leaves the room. I'm still in a bit of shock with how natural he is with her. I've never seen Paul with a child before, and it has done nothing but make him even sexier.

"I don't even know why Benson keeps putting his snacks up here. He thinks he's hiding them, but everyone knows they're up here," Sophie says as she tosses the package of cookies back up on the shelf.

We take our wine glasses and head into the living room. It feels so warm and cozy in here, which is difficult to do with such an open massive space. I'm sure the fire going helps with that cozy feeling. The windows have no treatments, but I can't see what's outside of them because it's so dark outside. I've heard it described, but I'm anxious for tomorrow's daylight.

The relaxing evening of girl talk and chatter was everything I had hoped it would be. Just like before, our conversations were easy. Laughter constantly filled the room. Daphne has amazing stories from her nights at the pub. Sophie shares many hilarious stories about being a mom. What feels like minutes has turned into hours later and the guys come up from the basement.

I'm still wiping the tears away from laughing so hard when Paul comes into view. He's not happy at all. Our laughter silences as each of us take in the faces of our men.

"What's going on?" Sophie asks.

"C'mon, sweets. Let's go to bed." Benson takes Sophie's hand. Reluctantly and looking worried, she takes it and heads out of the room.

I'm still scanning between Finn, Daphne, and Paul. Finn gives Daphne a look, then does a quick head nod toward the upstairs. She gets the hint and goes with him, too.

"Paul, what's happening?" I ask.

He sits on the coffee table in front of me and places his hands on my knees. My heart picks up pace. Whatever he's about to tell me isn't going to be good news.

"I got a call from Everest. You had flowers delivered to your parents' house today."

"Oh, I bet it was my mother. I told her about my new job."

Paul's eyes look to the floor briefly before returning to me. "It wasn't your mother. Whoever this Carter is sent them."

Frustrated, I blow out through my lips. "He's probably just trying to apologize for being an idiot…"

"No." Paul's voice is stern. "There was a note. Jo, I'm telling you. Even if you don't want to. I need you to trust me."

Now he's starting to scare me. The look on his face is far from the happy one he wore earlier. He is so alarmed that I don't say anything and just nod. A feeling of panic begins to rise inside of me. I look to the windows and then to the front door.

"Don't worry. Benson was showing me all of the security measures he's put into place here since there was a scare with Sophie. Every inch of his property has fence around it and is monitored constantly. You're safe here."

"What did the note say?" I ask quietly.

Paul pulls his phone out of his pocket and brings up an image of sloppy handwriting on a small florist card.

> *You looked amazing in that red dress.*
> *Unlike him, I won't give up.*
> *-Carter*

Chapter
Seventeen

—

Paul

The light blue color that paints the sky reminds me of Heather's eyes. Vibrant and so full of light. I don't think people really know what peaceful is until they've sat on a bench, at the foot of a mountain range, surrounded by trees. The green mountains look even more impressive with spring in bloom around them. If it weren't for these stones on the ground in front of me, it would be my favorite place on earth. It's so beautiful.

The last time I was here, I sat next to letters on a rock that spelled out Heather's name and watched her brother marry the love of his life. I was his best man. Even though I was so happy for him and it was such a great day, it felt like I didn't live up to my role. Best man. I sure didn't feel like a best man. I felt like the worst man. And seeing her name on that rock for the first time crushed whatever life I still had in me.

Now I'm on my knees before that same stone today, begging for forgiveness. For the ability to move on. For my heart back. My words float on the breeze and up to whoever is up there that might be listening. I loved Heather long before we became involved. Being best friends with her brother since we were young, she was always someone I cared about.

I knew Heather practically my entire life. The love I had for her was confusing and complicated. It got more complicated as the days went on until one day, it was too heavy. I couldn't hold all the weight that was on my shoulders and I had to put it down. My heart wasn't buried with Heather because she was the love of my life. I buried it here because I didn't trust myself enough to give it to anyone else. With a tear falling down my cheek, I utter the words she deserved all those years ago and never got. I'm sorry.

Movement from the tree line grabs my attention. My heart picks up pace as I see Jolene walking out of the woods toward me. Her hair is blowing in the breeze, and her hand covers her open mouth as she takes in the mountain view. The only time I ever feel alive is when she is near. I felt it the day after the wedding when I saw Jolene picking up takeout food. I dodged out of her view as she walked to her car. Her husband was sitting in the driver's seat on his phone waiting for her. She didn't look happy like I had pictured she was. I felt my chest lurch forward as she drove away. Then, nothing. Not until I saw her again that day at the pub.

An unexplained peace suddenly falls over me. Once Jolene has my eyes, they never leave her as she gracefully walks through the tall grass that surrounds the gravestones of Benson's family. My family. Her sweet vanilla scent touches me before she does. A sympathetic smile brightened by her red lips accompanies her hand on my shoulder. I didn't realize that I was still on my knees. She moves to the bench and sits without saying a word. She doesn't need to. I rise and sit next to her. Five small fingers wrap around my hand and there we sit. All of us. Together. I feel whole.

My mind travels back to the conversation from last night. I finally got through to Jolene about Carter. She's not a dumb woman. Her heart just wants to see the good in everyone, and I can't argue with that. It's the only reason she saw the good in me. But I had to tell her about Everest and his buddies. She really got scared when I told her that Everest has seen his vehicle drive past the condo multiple times. For some reason, Carter always seems to be just one step ahead of us. It's just too dangerous at this point, and even though the police make me extremely nervous, Jolene is going to file a police report when we get home. But for right now, she's safely tucked into my side and the sun is shining down on us.

"I wasn't prepared for the view when I walked into the living room this morning. It took my breath away." Her whispered voice barely breaks the silence.

"It is stunning. Benson has an eye for perfection. I think he nailed it with that house. His mother's favorite spot was out on the deck staring at the mountains."

"That's where I found Sophie this morning. Benson took the kids to get donuts for everyone, and Finn and Daphne were still asleep. I sat with her for a little while before coming to find you. She told me you would be here."

A smile crosses my face. I didn't tell Sophie I was coming out here. That woman just knows me.

"Are you ready to go back?" I ask her.

"Only if you are."

Taking a long, slow look from the mountains, to the trees, and to the place my heart used to be buried.

"Yep. I'm ready."

—

The rest of the day was spent relaxing together. Benson, Finn, and I ended up in a tea party in a room with pink walls. I'm pretty sure there was a picture taken from the three ladies laughing hysterically in the doorway. Once the evening came, Carol came down and babysat the kids so we could go out for a bit. We hit one of Benson and Sophie's favorite general stores, then walked down the sidewalks of the little town of Wellan. It was the first time I've been able to spend a long period of time with Benson, Sophie, Finn, and Daphne without feeling like I didn't belong. Like I was the fifth wheel.

Now that it's Sunday, and we're heading back home to Boston, the nerves are back up. Being at the mountain house, we were easily distracted from the problems at home. Jolene not only has the problem with Carter, but she's also still fighting with her parents. Dwight called her yesterday and told her he was coming home and that they were going to have a sit-down conversation. I know she's not looking forward to that.

Benson made a call into his buddy at the police station. He's there waiting for us to come in and make a report. I was very against going to the cops for any of this. But Benson and Finn talked me into it. Said it would help cover us in case something did happen and the police would have the report on file. We all know that it will still be up to us to find this asshole and put an end to his obsession with Jolene.

I squeeze Jolene's hand as it sits in mine on the center console in my car. Her mirrored sunglasses show the reflection of the city as it comes into view.

Chapter
Eighteen

—

Jolene

Scrubs. I wasn't sure if I would ever put them on again. After what happened with Myles, I didn't know what I was going to do. Just before I walk out of the door, I do a final check in the mirror so that I look my best on my first day in Dr. Ray's office. I asked Paul if Everest could drive me to and from work today. Not because I'm scared to drive myself—although maybe I am—but if I'm going to surprise Paul tonight, I'm going to need Everest's help.

Exiting the elevator into the lobby, Everest stands against the wall waiting for me. I smile in his direction, but his face barely moves. He walks right at my side all the way to the car and then opens the door for me.

"You know you don't have to open my door."

"Where I come from, mamas teach their boys to open a door for a woman."

Well, there isn't a whole lot I can argue with about that. I climb in and prepare to beg Everest to help me and keep a secret from Paul. I know how loyal Everest is, but I'm hoping he'll agree that Paul needs this.

"So. I need to ask you something."

"Aw shit," Everest mumbles as he runs his hand over his face.

"This afternoon after I get off work, I need to go to my friend Billie's house to pick up some things I bought for Paul's condo. It's a surprise, so you can't tell him."

"Keeping secrets from Paul isn't something I'm capable of doing."

"Oh come on. It's not like this is a secret he won't find out about. I bought some wall décor and a few pieces to make that place more like a home. That's it. He'll find out the minute he gets home tonight. Please?"

Everest huffs loudly.

"Fine. But I'm with you every step and there's no arguing. Until we get this situation figured out, if Paul isn't with you, I am. Got it?"

"Got it. There might be one other teensy little thing."

"Jesus. It gets worse."

"I might need your help carrying everything upstairs."

"You think I'd just stand there watching you carry everything yourself?"

There's just something about Everest that makes me laugh. He acts so grumpy, but you can tell he has a heart of gold. He really cares about Paul, and that shows with how much care he's taking with me.

"If Paul hates it, I had nothing to do with any of it."

"Deal," I say, smiling.

Everest parks the car and walks me all the way up to the door of the doctor's office. He doesn't leave until he watches me put his phone number into my phone.

"Text me when you're ready to go home. We'll meet right here and I'll walk you down to the car."

"Ugh. I filed a police report last night. You all following my every move is a bit ridiculous."

"No. It's smart."

"But I don't get it. Why not just let the cops do their jobs? I filed a report last night."

"The cops don't always get it right the first time." Everest turns to walk away. "Just ask Paul about that."

"What?" I shout after him. "What does that mean?"

As soon as Everest turns back around and I see the look on his face,

I can tell he didn't mean for me to hear that.

He shakes his head. "Not my place." Then he points to the office door, wanting me to go inside.

Rolling my eyes, I walk into the office. Even though I'm excited for this new position, I'm even more excited for the first day to be over. Not just because of those first-day jitters, but also because I couldn't be more anxious to do something for Paul. And now that I know Everest is on my side, we should be able to get it done way before Paul comes home from work.

———

"Can my place be next?" Billie teases, as she helps us load the last box into the car. "I'm obsessed with the big one that goes above the couch."

"That one is my favorite too. Thank you for letting me ship it all here and holding onto it."

"Of course. I'm just sorry I can't come help you hang it all up like I was supposed to. I had no idea that Sam had invited his mother for dinner tonight."

"It's not a big deal. Thanks again."

I give her a quick hug and she runs inside. Everest is still trying to adjust everything in the back of his car. The large box that contains the canvas to be hung behind his black leather couch barely fits. Once the trunk shuts, I nervously look to my watch.

"We better hurry, or I'm going to blow this whole thing."

It takes two trips to get everything up to Paul's condo. With everything piled in the living room, I turn to Everest, half out of breath.

"Thank you so much for helping me carry this up."

"Do you think I'm leaving?" He grabs a box and starts taking everything out. "You'll never get it done working alone. I'll take it all out and you put it where you want it."

I know this is the worst time to ask, but my curiosity is making me crazy. I go to ask and then hesitate.

"What?"

"It's rude. And none of my business."

"Just spit it out."

"What did you do?"

Confusion crosses his face, but it's brief. "Paul tell you he met me in jail?"

Shameful. Me and my big mouth. "Yes."

"Walked in on my mama's boyfriend hitting her. I killed him."

The words come out of his mouth as if he's said it a million times. Shock radiates through me. I'm standing in front of a killer. A killer is helping me decorate Paul's condo. Everest must see the fear that entered me as soon as he said those last three words.

"You have nothing to worry about with me. I'd never hurt a woman."

As my brain begins functioning again, I stand there analyzing his crime. He's not some cold-blooded killer. He was protecting his mother. I don't know many men that would stand by and watch that happen.

"Word of advice. Never ask a question you don't really want the answer to. Some will actually be honest."

He holds up a handful of candles that he just unwrapped from one of the boxes. Knowing that Paul would never put me in danger, and the fact that Everest has been protecting me for days now, I nod and take the candles.

It doesn't take long with Everest's help. We get everything put where I want it to go. I've tried to stay true to Paul's dark tastes. Different shades of black and gray were the main colors of my décor picks. The only touches of color I used in the living room were green plants. I got a few cacti plants for the side table and the island and a tall fiddle leaf fig tree that fits perfectly into the corner by the window. The largest piece of art I purchased was for above the couch. The canvas was covered in white, and the artist used gray and black to create the Boston skyline out of brush strokes. It was elegant, but still held onto the masculine feel of the room. If it wasn't for Everest, I never would have gotten that hung by myself. I got a few light gray pillows to contrast against the black leather couch.

A lot of the artwork I bought for the condo was from a discount home store. It's always been one of my favorite places to shop because they have prints for really cheap that are already in frames and ready to hang. This allowed me to get many more items to help make this empty condo look like a home.

I keep looking at the new clock we just hung up by the door and waiting for Paul to walk in. It feels like he's taking forever. With every minute that passes, I move something around. The glass hurricane candle holders that I placed on the coffee table have been rearranged five times. Unable to sit any longer, I begin walking around the condo rethinking the position of everything. Once I'm satisfied enough with the living room, I walk into the bedroom. So caught up in getting ready for Paul to come home, I tossed my scrubs on the floor when I changed. I want it to look perfect in here. Quickly, I grab them, run into Paul's walk-in closet where he keeps the laundry basket, and put them in. Just before I'm about to walk out, something catches my eye from the top shelf. A box decorated in gold and blue paper. My curiosity once again trumps my manners, and I carefully pull it down. My heart beats out of my chest as the tips of my fingers run over the letters written in beautiful curly cursive. *Heather Knoxx.* On an angle in the top corner was a torn off piece of paper that was covered in tape. It said, *Love, Paul.* Probably the bottom of a letter he wrote to her.

Everything inside of me is telling me not to open the box. None of this is my business. Ignoring the angel sitting on my right shoulder telling me to put the box back where I found it, I walk into the bedroom and sit on the bed. The front flap is connected with a magnet that easily releases as I pull it back. Inside, loose papers are shoved inside along with a thread bracelet, a pencil, and a heart pendant. I pick up a handful of papers and see that they are all diary entries. I quickly put it down before reading it. "This is wrong," I say out loud to myself and start putting the papers back in.

"What did you do?" Paul's voice billows through the bedroom. Paul stands in the middle of the doorway, arms crossed, and a stern look on his face.

With wide, horrified eyes, there's no excuse to be made. "I threw my clothes into the hamper. The gold caught my eye. The curiosity got the best of me. I know I shouldn't have looked in this. It's yours, and I'm sorry."

"I have nothing to hide from you, Jolene. I'm talking about all this stuff. What the hell did you do?"

Stunned, I can't get my focus off this box. "You're not upset I'm looking through this box?"

He shakes his head. "There's nothing in that box that you don't already know."

"Is there anything in here that explains why Wednesdays are so difficult?"

He takes a deep breath, sets his keys that were still in his hand on top of the dresser, and sits next to me on the bed. He pushes a stray hair behind my ear, and by the look in his eyes, he's having a hard time.

"There's a diary entry in there. She wrote it that morning after we had spoken and decided to meet. She wanted to get help so that I could love her again. I was trying to save her. Told her I would meet her at five, but I was late. She didn't wait for me. They found her that night in the alley. It was a Wednesday."

Listening to him makes my heart break. He's taken on so much of this pain.

"Let's put this away," I say. Picking up the box, I climb over him to get off the bed, but he grabs me just as my legs are on either side of him. He takes the box out of my hand and pulls me into him. The material of his suit is cool against my skin. He presses a kiss to my lips before pulling back again.

"We need to talk about the living room." His shoulders drop as he looks around the bedroom. He hadn't noticed it when he saw me on his bed with the box. "The bedroom, too."

"You hate it." I say, disappointed. "I just wanted to give you a warm place to come home to."

"I fucking love it."

"Then why did you look so mad when you walked in?"

"I was trying to control myself. Apparently, that doesn't do good things for my face."

He takes the box, closes it, and disappears into his closet. When he emerges, he's lost the suit. Something about the way his muscles dance across his body as he saunters my way makes me want to run my hands over them. He pushes my shoulder until I'm on my back. His biceps bulge as he holds himself directly above me.

"You did all this for me."

With anticipation, I lick my lip and nod.

"My turn to do something for you."

He places a kiss on my lips, then drags his tongue down the center of my neck until he reaches the center of my entire being. If I knew that buying him a few pictures was going to result in a full worship of my body with his tongue, I would have bought them a long time ago.

—

"Please, can we go through a drive-through and get a coffee?" I ask Everest on our way to work. I overslept this morning as Paul kept me up all night last night. Not that I'm complaining, but I have to be on my game today.

"You don't have time," he says.

I'm not sure when it happened. Maybe it was the day Everest took me to the pub and promised to keep me safe. Or maybe it was when we got real with each other while putting together Paul's surprise. But Everest and I have suddenly developed a sibling-like relationship. I've never had an older brother, but if I did, I would imagine the same kind of banter would ensue. Plus, it makes this entire nightmare a bit easier to take since Everest is following me around everywhere that Paul isn't.

"There's plenty of time. You just want to get rid of me. C'mon, my treat."

"I'm just bringing you to work. I'm not a damn chauffeur."

Thirty minutes later I wave at Everest as I walk into the doctor's office sipping on my coffee. I think he said no just to get a rise out of me. Then he wouldn't let me pay for it either. Lord knows I'm going to need this caffeine. Not only do I have to get through the day, but I'm going to talk to my father tonight. Paul rearranged his schedule to pick me up from work today so that he can take me to my parent's house. I don't want to fight with him. But I'm not going to let him dictate my life anymore. It will be up to him on how tonight goes. Until then, I just have to focus on my patients.

—

"Nervous?" Paul asks.

"Not really," I lie. "I just don't want to fight anymore. I'm exhausted with all of this."

"I'm going to be at the coffee shop with Everest just around the corner. I'm talking three minutes from here. When you want to leave, call me and I'll be here in three minutes."

"You mean you aren't going to be watching me blow my nose through the window," I tease.

A snicker comes from Paul as the pad of his index finger presses up against the bottom of my chin. "I have my issues with your father. But I know he loves you and wouldn't let anything happen to you. Besides, I'm minutes away."

He leans over the center console, puts his hand against my cheek, and kisses me.

"I love you," I tell him.

"Move in with me. The thought of walking into that condo without you makes me never want to go there again."

"Thank God," I sigh. "I don't want to be anywhere else."

"I love you, Fancy."

One more quick kiss, then I rush out of his car. He watches me as I go up to the door and my father opens it. I hear the car take off as the door closes and he knows I'm safely inside.

"Hi, Daddy," I say, rubbing my hands together nervously.

"Come here." He wraps me up in the same embrace that eased my fears for all these years. "I don't want to fight."

My shoulders drop in relief. I've always cherished the relationship with my father. But that doesn't mean that we don't butt heads sometimes. I know he isn't going to like the fact that I'm moving in with Paul, but he doesn't need to know that yet. Let's just try to get through this conversation without screaming at each other again.

My father makes small talk and asks me about my new job. He takes the opportunity to lecture me about the healthcare industry. Most of which I zoned out for. Everything seems like it's going fine. I ask about my mother. She didn't come to Boston with my father because she has a few events with her ladies club. We managed to talk for over an hour without fighting so I figure now is as good of a time as any to get some more of my things before I text Paul to come pick me up. While I'm upstairs, I hear someone at the door. My body stills, and I listen to see if my father knows who is there.

"Jolene..."

My father's voice suddenly cuts off, but I'm already halfway down the stairs.

"Daddy?" I take a few more steps, and the scene before me makes my blood freeze in my veins. My father is on the floor, blood coming from his head. A man with light brown hair stands next to him with some kind of metal rod in his hand. His crazed eyes look through me. An evil smile creeps across his face. Snapping out of it, I pull my phone from my pocket and begin running back up the stairs. I type in the four letters before a heavy weight falls on top of my body. My finger barely taps SEND before he grabs a handful of hair and jerks my head back in pain.

"Not wearing red today? Shame."

My mouth opens to scream, but nothing comes out and everything goes black.

Chapter
Nineteen
—

Paul

"His name is Nathaniel Carter Ray. He's an ex-cop. He started going by Carter after he was released from the department." Everest takes a drink of his coffee.

"That makes sense. Explains how he's been able to be one step ahead of us. He knows what he's doing," Gill says.

I feel like we were just here. All four of us, sitting around this table, planning how we were going to keep Jolene safe and find this guy. I never would have thought we would be dealing with someone so experienced on crime.

"You boys ready to explore tonight?" Everest asks.

Whack flashes a devilish smile, and Gill nods.

"Don't do anything to him," I warn. "Just make sure you have the right guy."

Whacks smile fades. "You take away all my fun."

My phone chimes, and I can't help but get a little excited. I'm so ready to get the hell out of here and take Jolene back to the condo. Back to our home, together. Only that feeling doesn't last. It's replaced by extreme fear. As I read the four letters on my screen, all of the blood drains from my face. *Help.* Everest grabs the phone out of my hands as I abruptly stand. Out of the corner of my eye, I see the chair hit the floor, but I don't hear a thing. There was no sound as my three friends got up from the table and began running toward the door. Frozen. My feet, my body, my heart, all frozen in place.

"Paul. Move," Everest orders. I finally come undone from my spot when he yanks on my arm and begins pulling me to the door. Once outside he hits a button on his key fob, unlocking the doors on his car, and the four of us jump in. Everest hands me back the phone and I immediately dial Jolene. *Pick up, Fancy. Just pick up the fucking phone.* No answer. I hang up and call again. With each passing minute, my fists ball up tighter on my lap. Anger takes over, and it violently rages inside. That ice fades away, and it's replaced with flowing lava.

"Fuck!" I scream, unable to hold it in any longer.

"We're right here, man," Gill says as we pull up to the brownstone. From the outside, everything looks fine. Everest doesn't even have the car in park yet, but Gill, Whack, and I are already jumping out. I bust through the unlocked front door and see red. There's a small amount of blood on the carpet, but my attention goes to the couch. The couch that I laid Jolene down on the night she came back and gave me life. The guys charge past me, looking in the first floor rooms. I shake the thoughts out of my head and bolt up the stairs. Jolene's bedroom door is open and inside, clothes are strewn about the bed next to a suitcase. She was in the middle of packing up her things. Her purse sits half open on the bed, and something from inside catches my eye. Pulling it out, I stare at the four-by-six photo of the two of us at the gala. My fancy girl in that stunning dress. I take it with me and continue checking all the rooms upstairs but find nothing.

"They took Dwight Barrington's car," Gill yells from the back door that leads to the garage.

We all run into the kitchen where Gill stands holding open the door to the garage. He points to a spot of blood on the ground leading to the garage. "I watched Dwight pull his car into this garage before I left to meet you at the café. It's gone now."

"Let's go," Everest orders.

Back in the car, I text Benson and Finn. Benson responds that he's on his way and Finn will handle the cops. I'm sure they're going to want to talk to me, but there's no way in hell I'm letting them delay me from finding Jolene. There's a difference between us finding her and them finding her. They have to follow certain procedures. We don't.

The fifteen-minute drive to the suburb of Boston where Gill has pegged this asshole lives is the longest car ride I've ever taken. The neighborhood looks like one I wish I could have grown up in. Far from the picture I had created in my mind of dilapidated houses with bars on the windows. With darkness overtaking the light, most homes have interior lights on. A large picture window shows a family gathered around the dinner table. They probably have no clue there's a dangerous man living only doors down. Everest slows, and Gill points to a two-story house with light yellow siding. There are no lights showing anything inside. I reach for the handle ready to jump out when Whack grabs my arm.

"No," he says, shaking his head.

"Fuck you, Whack."

"You gotta be smart."

"He's right, Paul. Look up there," Gill says, and points out the security camera focused on the front door. "He'll see you as soon as you go up to that house."

"So what the fuck do we do? Sit here and waste time while God knows what is happening to Jolene?"

"We park a few blocks down. I was already planning on checking this place out tonight with Whack, so I brought a laser. I'll walk ahead of you, and when I get close enough, I'll shine a laser into the camera, which will make it useless. Then you run up and do your thing."

I have no idea if Gill's plan is going to work, but I couldn't care less. I want to rush this house. Dwight's car is nowhere in sight, but it's possible it could be in the garage, or he ditched it somewhere and picked up his own car. Everest pulls into an empty spot on the side of the road around the corner from the house. We give Gill a few feet of space and follow him up to the house. He stops, points his laser at the house, and then motions us to move forward. Careful not to get in the path of the laser, we rush up to the house. The windows are all closed up with curtains, so there's no seeing inside.

"Only one thing to do," Whack whispers. "Whack," he says as his body slams into the front door, busting it open. I guess we know where Whack got his name from.

Everest pulls a hand gun out of his waistband. He was a skilled marksman in the military before he landed himself in jail. He keeps it at his side as we look around the space. The inside of the house looks nothing like the outside. The smell of garbage is overwhelming. It lays all over the counters and floor. There's old, worn-out furniture and a TV in the living room, but I'd be shocked if someone actually sat in here to watch it. Truthfully, it looks like no one has been here in quite some time. The three of us make quick work looking through the rooms for Carter and Jolene. All of our heads turn as a noise comes from under us. The basement. Everest finally opens a door that leads to the basement. With each step down I take, thunder hits me in the chest. I'm scared of what I might find, and when my feet hit the concrete floor, the sight makes me want to throw up. Nothing. There's fucking nothing here. She's not here. The light that Jolene brought back into my life is slowly dimming. The dark swallowed me whole and held me there for years with no hope of escaping it. I won't be able to face that dark again. It won't just swallow me this time, it will take the last thread I was holding onto and strangle me with it.

"Fuck," Everest says, running his hand over his forehead and down the back of his head.

We have nothing. She's not here and we don't know where he took her. I know she's still alive. My heart is still beating, which means so is hers. Everest puts a hand on my shoulder and I turn to him.

"If she dies, I die."

Chapter
Twenty

—

Jolene

Like a strobe light in a dark room, my surroundings slowly come into view as my eyes blink rapidly. The throbbing in my head radiates through my entire body. Get it together, Jolene. This nightmare worsens as the room around me comes into focus. The musty smell of an old, unoccupied house turns my stomach sour. What looks like old newspapers show through the peeling wallpaper on the four walls of the tiny room. As I look over my shoulder, the door that has me trapped inside is behind me. I'm sitting on a hard wood chair, my hands tied behind the back. My blush pink scarf that my mother bought me on my birthday sits tightly in between my teeth and around my head.

I listen for any sound of movement but hear nothing. The house is completely still. My wrists are burning, but I begin trying to work the knot with my fingers. It feels impossible, but I won't stop trying. Remembering my father laying on the ground, obviously struck in the head by this man, only intensifies the tears streaming down my face. *Is he dead? Did this lunatic kill my father just to get to me?* The last few weeks rush through my mind. The fights I've had with my daddy and the terrible things I've said to him. Then my thoughts turn to Paul and I can't help but think about what this is going to do to him. If I don't make it out of here, how is he going to move on? How is he ever going to learn to love again? My heart splits right down the center for both of them. My chin falls down to my chest as the sobs become harder to control.

"I wouldn't do that if I were you."

A startling voice from behind makes my heart beat rapidly. Two hands press firmly down on my shoulders as the heat from his body presses against the back of the chair. It's a struggle to keep the contents of my stomach down, but I fight against the nausea. The scarf in my mouth doesn't allow me to swallow properly and is causing saliva to wet my chin.

Carter pulls on the rope, and it bites into my flesh. An unconscious, small cry falls from my mouth.

"Shut up."

"Why are you doing this?" I try to ask, but it all comes out as a mumble.

His heavy boots make a low sound against the hardwood floor with each step. Once he's in front of me, he kneels down until our eyes are even. I notice the butt of a gun sticking out of his waistband. But I'm desperate for answers. I can't help but to keep asking questions even if he doesn't understand them through the material in my mouth.

"Where's my father? Is my father dead?" A tear falls from my lash, and the sensation of it slowly falling down my cheek gives me a shiver.

"Is your father dead? Is that what you asked me?"

I nod, full of terror that his answer is going to be what I think it will.

"No." His face tightens, and he looks at me like I'm the one who's crazy. "I wouldn't kill an innocent man."

My head again falls to my chest from the relief that my father is still alive. I try to ask another question, but this time, he doesn't understand me. An annoyed groan fills the room as he looks at me with confusion. He pulls the fabric out of my mouth so hard that my head jerks forward and pain sears through me again. I take a deep breath in and swallow like my body has begged to do since I woke up.

"If you're not going to kill us, then what do you want? Money?"

The laugh that comes from deep within him reminds me of something out of a horror film. "I said I wouldn't kill him. He's innocent. Nothing came out of my mouth about not killing you. You're guilty."

"Guilty?" I squeal, the cry of fear in my voice.

He nods. "I'm a cop. Did you know that? My job is to take care of the bad guy."

I shudder as his hand strokes down my cheek, wiping away the moisture from the tears. Revolted by his touch, I twist my head in the opposite direction. I hear the sound of the slap before the sting hits my face.

"You're the bad guy," he says, his expression dark and cruel. Still trying to regroup from the slap to my cheek, I'm slow at taking in one more good breath before he shoves the scarf back into my mouth and readjusts the tightness. He stands, gives me one more appalled look, then walks out of the room.

The bad guy? How am I the bad guy? I'm trying to focus on the fact that he assured me my father is alive. I know Paul is going to be looking for me. He's going to have every man he knows looking for me. So there's hope, and I have to hold onto that. But Carter's heavy boots continue to make sound from beyond the door behind me. The noise gets louder and heavier. Turning my ear in the direction of the door, I'm desperate to hear what is happening. The door bursts open, and my father, bound and gagged, is dragged into the room and tossed to the floor. He's alive.

"Jolene!" My name is easily understood through the material he also has tied around his face.

"Say goodbye," Carter says to my father.

He violently shakes his head. Desperately, he pleads for my life.

"I didn't get to say goodbye," he says. "I don't think that's very fair. I'm giving you the chance. You better take it while you can."

Carter's head flicks quickly to the dust-covered window. A streak of light ran across from right to left. Without another word, he runs out of the room and shuts the door behind him. My father begins moving his head in all directions, fighting to get the material out of his mouth. The tears fall from his eyes as he looks at me, finally freeing from the fabric.

"I'm so sorry," he whispers. "I'm so sorry, Jolene. This is all my fault. I did this."

"No," I cry through the scarf.

"Yes. I told Carter where to find you. I met him at the hospital the day before I retired."

My father's admission doesn't make any sense. My brain begins working in overdrive to try to comprehend everything he's telling me. But it just doesn't make sense.

"He was a stand-up guy. A police officer. Came from a good family. I knew you would never go on a date that I recommended."

"No," I cry. "Daddy, no."

"You need to know. I can't live with myself not telling you the truth. I told him about that app. I told him about the gala. I told him you were coming over tonight."

"Why?" I grunt.

The strongest man I've ever known lays there, helpless on the ground, his face full of sorrow and grief.

"To get you away from Paul."

I have no words that could even come close to the mix of emotions I feel. My father has been feeding information to this guy on my whereabouts. He knew exactly where I would be all the time. My vision blurs as my eyes flood with water until the tears overflow, rewetting my face.

A slow clap from behind me pulls our attention to the doorway. Carter leans against the frame, clapping.

"Coming clean?" he says to my father. Carter walks to my father on the ground and squats down low next to him. "But you didn't tell her the best part."

My father shakes his head. His eyes full of both anger and fear. My confusion rises, and I feel like this all has to be some horrible nightmare.

"I bet he didn't tell you everything," he says, amused. "See, he hates your little boyfriend so much that he blackmailed him to break up with you."

"No," I say in disbelief.

"Oh yeah. Funny story. Paul was charged with larceny, only he didn't steal anything. His mother did. Paul took the wrap. And your old man knew all about it. Threatened Paul that he would turn his mother in if he didn't stay away from you."

The blood is still flowing through my veins, but at this moment, I feel already dead. I know how much my father hated Paul. He always told me to stay away from him. That he was a criminal. It was my father the whole time. My poor Paul. He was so broken and no wonder. He hadn't failed anyone. Everyone failed him. The rage building inside of my chest is more than I can bear. My hands shift through the pain of the rope, desperately trying to get free. I need to get free for Paul. And I need to get free for me. I've been trapped in this charade for years and didn't even know it. My father, the one man I had always trusted and counted on, has handed to me the ultimate betrayal.

"I don't understand why you are doing this," my father asks Carter.

Carter pivots on his toes and gets so close to my face that his breath is hot on my skin.

"Because Myles was my brother. And instead of doing her job"—I jump as Carter yells the last word and his saliva hits my face as he speaks—"she let him die on the floor in that hospital."

His cold eyes peer into mine as I realize what this is about. He wants revenge. And his revenge is me dead. A loud noise from outside alerts Carter, and he lunges out the door, leaving my father and me in the room. Shattered. I feel completely obliterated. But the anger from what my father has done is helping me. It's given me the adrenaline rush I need to power through the pain of the ropes. Carter must not be as good as he thinks he is because I get the knot loose and slip my hands out. Watching the door, I quickly pull and tug at the rope on my feet until they are free. Once I pull the scarf out of my mouth and toss it off of my head, I run to my father and begin working the knots around his wrists. I might be furious with him, I might even hate him right now, but I can't leave him here. And if either of us are going to get out of here alive, it's going to take more than just me.

Voices. I can't make out what they are saying, but I hear voices. A smile caused by disbelief that maybe, just maybe, someone found us. The door swings open and, out of fear, I fall backward. A large body moves in my direction, but from this side of the room, the only light is the illumination from the moon. As soon as the light hits his face, I jump at him.

"Jesus Christ, Everest. Thank God," I whisper.

He doesn't say anything and puts his finger over his lips, telling me to shut up. Moving in the direction of my father, he pulls out a blade and cuts the ropes from his hands. Before Everest can cut the rope from my father's ankles, he stops him.

"Get her out of here," he says to Everest. "Get my daughter out of here and get her safe."

Their eyes communicate something that I don't understand, and before I can argue, Everest hands the knife to my father, tosses me over his shoulder, and races out of the room.

I don't want to leave my father. This psychopath could kill him. But as we get into the hallway, I hear Carter's voice and I grip onto the back of Everest's shirt. I've never been so scared in my entire life than the minute I woke up in that room and Carter walked in. We move in the opposite direction from the voices until suddenly the fresh air from outside hits my face. Everest's large body doesn't seem to have any problems running at full force while carrying a grown woman. His shoulder digs into my abdomen with each hop of his fast stride. He stops, grabs my hips, and places me down on my feet. A bright flashlight shines in my eyes for a minute before moving to another part of my face.

"It's going to be okay, Ms. Jolene," the man says.

"This is Gill. He's one of us. You can trust him. Stay with Gill. He'll keep you safe."

"My father," I begin, but Everest interrupts me.

"I'll get him," he says.

"Where's Paul?" I ask.

The two men look at each other, then back to me. I don't like the look in their eyes.

"Where is he?"

"He's making sure you're safe," Everest says.

Panic again takes over all other emotions. He must have been one of the muffled voices I heard in the house. He's in that house and I can't lose him.

"You've got to get him out, Everest. Carter's got a gun. It was in his waistband."

"Noted," he says. Then he turns around and bolts across the street toward the house we just came out of.

I hear sirens off in the distance. And Gill nods.

"Don't worry, Ms. Jolene. Everything is going to be all right."

Just as Gill gets out the last word, the echo of a gunshot rings in my ears. *Oh my God.*

Chapter
Twenty-One

—

Paul

"Hang in there. Keep looking at me."

"I'm sorry," Dwight says, his voice weak. "I'm sorry for everything."

I nod so that he knows I believe him. Blood begins to soak through the shirt I took off to keep pressure on the wound. We've hated each other for so long, and what he has done to me and my family has torn me apart. But as he lays on the floor, his blood on my hands, I know he's full of remorse.

Another scuffle from the corner gains my attention, but only to witness the sheer power that is Whack. He's holding Carter down on the ground and his arms wrapped tightly around Carter's neck. If those cops don't get in here fast, he's going to kill him just for the fun of it. The amused look on his face hasn't left since he tackled Carter after trying to shoot me. That gun was pointed right at me and the bullet inside had my name on it. Until Dwight jumped in front of the bullet. He saved my life. The life he wanted so badly to destroy for all these years.

"Why did you do it?" I ask Dwight.

"You saved her when I threw her to the wolf. I've been ignoring the truth. Her eyes lost their shine the day you left. The day I made you leave. You didn't break her heart, I did. I couldn't do it again. She loves you," he pauses, tears running down his face. "And I love her."

"I know. I know you do."

I hear Everest talking to a cop just outside the front door when three others rush into the house. They take Carter from Whack, cuff him, and walk him out. That's when Whack loses the gleam in his eye and his expressions returns to the bored look he wears every day.

"Just keep doing what you're doing, sir," one of the cops say. "Paramedics are pulling up now."

Dwight looks pale from the blood loss, but he's still conscious. All I can think about is Jolene and seeing her face. I have to see her face to know she's okay. Dwight told me that Everest got her out, but nothing is going to ease my fears until I press her against me and feel her heartbeat against mine. I know Gill will keep her safe and calm until I can get there.

A frenzy of movement catches my eye from the doorway and the paramedics rush to Dwight's side. They ask me a few quick questions before taking over caring for him. I stand back and give them the room they need. One police officer takes me to the side opposite of Whack and begins asking me questions about what went down. I answer as fast as I can because the only thing on my mind right now is getting to Jolene. They're going to have a lot of questions for her, and I want to be near her when she has to relive this horror.

With Dwight on the gurney and the paramedics raising it onto the wheels, his head tilts to the side and he stares at me. He's trying to say something, but I can't hear him. I lean closer to him, ignoring the question I was just asked by the cop.

"Tell her," he begs. "Tell her I'm sorry. Tell her…tell her Daddy loves her."

The water begins to puddle in the bottoms of his eyes. And without another word, they roll him out of the house. Even with my conflicted feelings, and being unsure how I feel about a higher power, I find myself internally praying for his life.

As the time passes, I begin to get nervous about where Jolene is. Once our statements are complete, I race out of the door and find Everest finishing up his statement with the police that have gathered outside. Whack pats my back like we just won a baseball game.

"Glad it all worked out for you, brother. I'm out."

Everest meets us at the bottom of the stairs.

"Hold up," he tells Whack, then walks up to me. "I want to be there."

"Where?" I ask, confused.

"If you don't marry this girl, I'm gonna be real pissed."

I want to laugh. I know that Everest can have a dry sense of humor, but there's a seriousness to his voice. He smacks my bicep then walks away with Whack.

There's so much activity and flashing lights. I begin rapidly scanning every single face until a familiar one catches my eye. Finn. He's facing two police officers while they talk. His large arms are wrapped tightly around Daphne, whose arms are wrapped tightly around Jolene. The same time my eyes hit her face, her eyes hit mine.

"Oh God," she cries and fights against the tight hold. Finn doesn't let go of the women until he spots me. His face is full of concern but also relief. Her strides are long, but not nearly as long as mine. My need to feel her is greater than any pain that could come from pushing my legs to their limits. Our bodies collide, and she jumps up on me. I grip her body so tightly against mine as she wraps her legs around my waist. The steady thunder from her chest hits against my skin. Her fingertips dig into my skin from how hard she's trying to hold onto me. I'm trying to let the relief beat down the rage that soared when I saw the marks on her face.

"Your dad,"

"I know," she whispers. "They told me."

Finn and Daphne approach us, but Jolene doesn't even think about letting go. Her head just lays down on my shoulder. I can understand how exhausted she must be and what it feels like when all the adrenaline begins to disperse. I had texted Finn the address before we broke into the house to rescue Jolene. I knew he would fill the cops in, but I was surprised to see him here.

"Thank you," I tell Finn, and he knows how serious I am. He nods. "Where's Gill?"

"Took off as soon as I got here. He said he doesn't do cops."

I don't think Gill will ever get back to a normal life. His trust issues are worse than mine but for good reason.

"Honey, are you okay?" Daphne asks Jolene's back. She still hasn't let go of me and I'm not about to let go of her. Daphne rubs Jolene's back, and she nods.

"I'm going to be." The quiet whisper from my girl makes me want to kill him. It makes me regret keeping Whack at bay.

"We should get going. Finn, can you take us to the hospital?"

"Let's move," he says.

———

Listening to the phone call Jolene had to make to her mother was excruciating for all of us in that truck. Having to hear even the diluted version of what happened almost makes me go crazy. If Jolene wouldn't have been smashed into my side, I'm not sure I would've been able to control my anger. But she needed me to. Just like she still needs me to.

After she was checked out by the doctor and the back of her head cleaned and we received instructions on how to handle her concussion, we sat waiting for what felt like an eternity in the waiting room. Daphne and Finn refused to leave us there until we got word that Jolene's dad was going to be okay. Jolene was able to go see him briefly, and then she demanded that we go home. She got no argument from me. Finn brought us back to the condo and, as we walked in the door, Jolene completely broke.

I carried her into the bedroom, took off her clothes, and laid her in bed. With my chest still wet from her tears and the sun shining brightly through the blinds, her breath finally evens out and she sleeps.

My mind tries to wander to the dark place. The place where I think about what today would be like if Jolene wasn't here. If I wasn't able to find her. If I didn't trust Everest with everything and go with his gut feeling. He found a bunch of mail with the same address. We flew out the door with the mail in hand. On the way, Gill did a little research and discovered the name on the mail was Carter's brother. The address belonged to Myles Ray. He also found a few newspaper articles about Myles' death and the connection it had with a gang member Carter had arrested previously. Carter was fired from the police department after being arrested for driving under the influence while on duty. Apparently, he had been having problems ever since his brother died. That moment, it all came together. That was when I was ready to do whatever I had to do to make sure Jolene would be okay. Even if that meant putting myself at the end of a killer's gun.

Feeling the gentle rhythm of her heart on my side, I push those thoughts away. We both deserve so much more than what we've been given. Now we focus on the happy. With gentle movements, I inch closer to the dresser on my side of the bed, reach into the drawer, and pull out the ring I bought for her all those years ago but never had the chance to give her. I went into the pawn shop with the money I got from working with Benson's dad. I slip it onto her finger and know that when she opens her eyes, the bad will be gone.

I snuggle down into the comforter and, with Jolene safe in my arms, I close my eyes.

—

Her hair, porcelain white flows back and forth in the breeze. The light illuminates her outline. *No. Not again.* The road, long and narrow in front of me. I don't want to run. I know what happens and it kills my heart every time. Her beautiful arm stretches behind her, in my direction, and I know the minute I reach for it, I will fail. But I can't stop myself. My eyes close and I reach forward, only to feel my hand enclosed in warmth. I open my eyes and she turns around. Jolene's stunning golden eyes stare back at me.

The next thing I know, I'm sitting upright in bed. My chest rising and falling so fast and Jolene's hand touching my arm.

"Are you okay? What's the matter? Did you have a nightmare again?" She quickly assesses me and places her hand against my chest.

"It wasn't a nightmare," I blurt. "Oh my God. It wasn't a nightmare." I bolt out of bed and begin pacing back and forth in the room. My mind scurrying to put it all together.

"Paul, you're scaring me."

"No. You don't understand." I rush to her. "It wasn't a nightmare. It never was."

With her hand again pressed firmly against my chest, I watch as her eyes land on the piece of jewelry I placed on her finger.

"What is this?" she asks, her voice cracks with emotion.

I stand from the bed, pulling her up with me. My lips press against hers as my heart beats wildly. Never breaking eye contact, I slowly fall to one knee.

"What are you doing?"

Her words barely come out as the smile covers her face and tears flow down.

"What I should have done a long time ago. I know you've been through hell. But I promise to never let you feel pain and heartache again. I bought you this ring when I was eighteen years old, and I've been dreaming of grabbing your hand and putting it on ever since. Marry me."

"My answer now is the same it would have been back then," she cries. "Yes."

Shooting up from the floor, I pick her up and spin her around. A giggle escapes her as I set her back on her feet.

"It's stunning," she says, holding her hand out and looking at the ring. The vintage setting props up the round diamond with swirls of gold that wrap around the band. It wasn't the most expensive ring, but I knew the second I saw it, it was perfect.

"Did you pick this out all by yourself?"

"I walked in and asked them for the fanciest one they had."

That sweet blush comes over her face as she angles her eyes up at me. "To match my fancy red dress?"

"No. To match the fancy white one."

The End.

Books By
C.E. Johnson

—

In the Dark Series
Done (In the Dark, #1)
Just One (In the Dark, #2)

Standalone
RAIN

Want more of my shenanigans? Join my reader group!
Reader group: C.E.'s Reading Roses http://bit.ly/CEsReadingRoses

Before
You Go

—

Please consider leaving an honest review. Reviews help authors, but
they also help readers like you to discover new books.
Thank you for reading!

About The
Author

—

C.E. Johnson is an author of contemporary and suspense romance novels. When not writing until all hours of the night (with lots of late-night coffee runs), she loves to read books that rip your heart out completely, then kindly place it back into your chest with a HEA.

A lover of winter, doggies, and things that sparkle.

She lives in a suburb of Chicago with her husband, two kids, and some spoiled, rotten animals.

PLEASE VISIT ME AT:

Website:
www.authorcejohnson.com

Facebook: @AuthorCEJohnson
https://www.facebook.com/authorcejohnson

Twitter: @AuthorCEJohnson
https://twitter.com/AuthorCEJohnson

Instagram: AuthorCEJohnson
https://www.instagram.com/authorcejohnson

Goodreads: AuthorCEJohnson
https://www.goodreads.com/AuthorCEJohnson

Made in the USA
Monee, IL
10 May 2022